# From WTF to OMG

### With a little LOL

DAVID CORBIN

KERRY JACOBSON

From WTF to OMG
With a little LOL
Unpacking Life's Hidden Lessons
David Corbin and Kerry Jacobson

Copyright © 2022
ISBN 979-8-9865632-3-7

Sigma Press

All rights reserved. No part of this book can be copied in any format, electronically, digitally, or otherwise, without consent of the publisher.

The content of this book is for informational purposes only. Neither the authors nor the publisher are liable for any damages whatsoever stemming from the content herein.

Printed in the United States of America

# INTRODUCTION

## David M. Corbin

WTF?

What the Fudge? What the Fertilizer?

You know what we mean when we ask, "What the F is going on here?"

The potty mouth F word can be substituted with many other adjectives, yet everyone knows what the F you're talking about.

And the W word? Well, as you can see, it's WHAT the F? In this book, we invite you to consider that the W also stands for WHY. WHY the F? It's a question, an inquiry, a search.

And that's really what this book is about. It's about asking your higher power, or the Universe, or God, or Vortex, or some such higher energetic power the WHAT and WHY about the crappy situation at hand; you know, specifically any situation that is painful, problematic, scary, and sometimes traumatic … where you instinctively say or think WTF?

We all have situations like this. Most of the time, we process them through the gristmill of our life, and then we just move on. Some situations take longer to get through than others. Some seem to never be resolved. Yet our research reveals that most of these situations tend to harbor within them a significant gift or lesson for us, a learning and sometimes even a profound transformation opportunity. But we also discovered that most people sure as hell didn't hold that positive expectation while in the midst of it … because, as they tell us, they felt various degrees of the S word: SUCK.

Happily, however, these situations seem to show up in our lives to instruct us on our path and not to obstruct us.

Over the past four years, we've asked literally hundreds of individuals about their experiences with this process, and most say that they have had many, many such WTF experiences … only to realize at some point in the future, "OMG-that happened for a reason," or "I never would have _____ (grown, achieved, realized, learned, created) _____ if not for that crappy experience." In other words, each situation that was WTF? actually had an embedded OMG! lesson or gift. And so often we heard the glorious LOL, that chuckle that comes with realizing that, for any number of reasons, we almost missed discovering and receiving the gift. Or the LOL because we are so loved and supported by those higher forces. From WTF? To OMG! With some LOL!!! You got it.

As you think about some of your personal WTF to OMG stories, we invite you to read some of ours: stories about being stuck in space, literally, or about living through a stroke only to discover an unrelated and potentially fatal brain aneurism, a speaker and writer told he can no longer speak or hold a pen, a story by an Olympian who was totally freaked out, and another story about losing a business but gaining a life. There's even one about living with Elvis at Graceland … and many more in which the author, like you, walked through the valley of darkness and came out of it with significant illumination and often profound lessons that they unpacked. Unpacked? Yes, they consciously or unconsciously searched for and discovered their lesson. And most of them expressed to us that they wish that they had assumed, in real time, during the shitstorm, that there was an embedded lesson—that they would have compressed the timeline to that lesson realization. They tell us that they now "expect" the gift within.

Here's some of the rhetoric around this topic and, frankly, it's germane.

The paranoid believes that the world conspires to hurt them.

The INVERSE paranoid believes that the world conspires to help them—thus they instinctively believe that the painful experience is part of the process of the world conspiring to help them, and they immediately begin the process of unpacking just how it is going to bless them.

Here's some more.

You remember that story about the optimistic child—the one who expects the best in all things—and when confronted with a huge pile of poop, says, "Well, there's got to be a pony in there somewhere!"

Oh, and here's another. You may have heard this one from a pretty well-known book where it is written, "Seek and ye shall find, ask and you will receive, knock and the door shall be opened."

Got it? Yeah, you got it.

So, after reading the many stories in this book, it is the intent of all of the contributing story authors that you know, really know, to remain open to and begin to "unpack the hidden lessons within," which is also this book's subtitle.

We, Kerry Jacobson and David Corbin, had the honor of curating these stories. Most of the authors are friends, colleagues, or at least acquaintances. It came as no surprise to us that each had many of these WTF to OMG stories to choose from. It was a trip to try to select the one story that really blessed their lives because there were so many. David and the authors discussed them on Zoom and when the time was right, pressed the record button. Then the recording went to Patti McKenna, writer extraordinaire, who wrote each story in a way and manner that speaks it most effectively … and voila.

We hope you catch yourself wondering *WTF?* as you read along, and then find yourself saying OMG! when the not-so-obvious gift comes to light and leaves you in awe. You might even LOL a little. We know we did.

Enjoy.

Davidcorbin.com

david@davidcorbin.com

# SWIMMING WITH A COW

## Neary Heng

Granted, to most people, standing in an open rice field while war planes are flying overhead would be considered a bad day. Sure, it's not like most people's typical bad days, but at that time in my life, it was typical enough that I knew what was happening and what I needed to do, even at a very young age. We've all had bad days. You know the type. You wake up late, spill coffee on your favorite shirt, get stuck in traffic, or drop your iPhone and crack the screen. I have those days, too. But when I do, I step back and realize that they are just inconveniences—small, insignificant events that only have the power to wreck my day if I let them. In the grand scheme of the vast universe, they are just a grain of sand among the things that will shape our lives.

Everyone has had experiences that transform their lives—things that actually shape much more than how we view our day, but instead, provide us with a different perspective on life. My childhood provided me with many such experiences, and although they weren't anything I'd actually wish for, I wouldn't trade any of them for a different life. The lessons I learned through those experiences have, in fact, led me to the life I live today—a big life full of gratitude, joy, happiness, prosperity, and health.

I think our perspective on life is modeled from our experiences. What may seem trivial and unimportant to some may seem monumental and catastrophic to others, depending on their previous experiences and life circumstances. A person who has had an easy life might be devastated when their bank account falls below six figures, while a person who has had hardships might feel grateful to be able to pay their bills. It's all about perspective, which comes from life lessons.

My first lesson actually came at a very young age. I was five years old and carrying out one of my tasks. In Communist controlled Cambodia, children were expected to do chores, not just at home, but for the government. One of my "jobs" was to bring the cows to their grassy feed area.

Our home was in an area where there were days when the sky seemed to dump its kidneys all at once, resulting in torrential downpours. Scientifically, it's called a monsoon. But from an observer's standpoint, it's basically a large outdoor swimming pool. There is standing water everywhere, and everything you can see or touch is soaking wet. We've all seen puddles, but monsoons left puddles the size of Texas. There is no escaping them or going around them. One literally has to swim through them.

When the ground is covered with water and the earth is saturated to the hilt, grass cannot grow. So I had to cross the river of water to take the cow I was in charge of to grassy land. It wasn't an easy task for anyone, especially a five year old. Now, I could have gotten out of it by lying and saying I fed the cow, like when a child tells a little fib and says they brushed their teeth, but they didn't. But I knew better. I was responsible for the cow and feeding it was my job. The cow wasn't owned by my family or a neighbor. It was owned by the government. One might think that the government wouldn't know or care whether the cow missed one feeding. Tell that to a five year old who likens their government to the mafia. When you mess with them, they will mess with you. I had that fear and wasn't about to test my luck. I was going to feed that cow, come hell or high water (no pun intended). If I didn't, I feared they would "take care of" me or my family. That's a lot for a young girl to shoulder.

So I set off with my cow and started our trek across the river. I might have omitted one small detail—I didn't know how to swim. I was afraid of the water. As I stood on the bank of the river, it was impossible not to notice the strong current as the swollen river rushed downstream. I looked across toward the grass and gauged my distance. Beyond frightened, I knew I was in trouble, but I also knew what I had to do. The cow wanted grass—I wanted to live. I very much wanted to quickly cross the river and be done with this job, but instead, I froze. Panicked, I couldn't bring myself to move. The cow, on the other hand, was a little smarter … and a lot braver than me.

The cow knew that it could swim. Unfortunately, the cow was the only one with that inside information. I had no clue that it could swim until it started swimming across the river. Left behind, I knew I had to act quickly! I couldn't lose the cow; it didn't belong to me—it belonged to the government, and I didn't want to mess with them. So I did the only thing I could do—I grabbed the cow by the tail and hung on for dear life.

Have you held on to the tail end of the cow? Well, let me tell you, the smell is not very pleasant. But it was better than the alternative, which was dying. So while I was trying to feed the cow and care for it, it was inadvertently saving my life. I'm sure the scene would have been hilarious to onlookers. Sometimes, I even imagine what it must have looked like from the sky—a helicopter flying overhead and its pilot doubled over in laughter as he watched a little five-year-old Cambodian girl floating down the river as she was hanging onto a swimming cow. At the time, though, there was nothing humorous about it. I had no idea where the cow was going or where it would take me. Obviously, the cow did—and truthfully, even if it didn't, there was nothing I could do about it.

The cow obviously had its GPS on and found where it needed to go—it must be a natural instinct for animals to find food, even if they have to go over the river and through the woods. I don't think I was ever so relieved as I was when the cow stepped onto the bank. Solid land! I was ecstatic to be alive, and judging by the way the cow thrashed its tail back and forth, it was just as glad that I had let go.

I was safe, for the time being, but I was still scared. I was wet, cold, and my legs were weak. Sinking to the ground, I sat and watched the cow calmly and leisurely eat its lunch, as if nothing had happened. But I knew something had happened, and my mind replayed the events one more time while I waited.

What happened? Well, I did my job and saved myself from drowning and punishment by the government. But something even bigger than that happened. I learned a lesson, but it wasn't until I was older, in my teens, that I truly realized what that lesson was. It was one of those lessons that stays with you for life—there's no doubt in my mind that I'll take it to my grave. That lesson is SBCI, an acronym for Stop, Breathe, Center, and Inventory.

Let me explain. Whenever I'm confronted with a challenge, regardless how big or small it is, I stop. I stop everything and avoid any temptation to fix the situation. I remove myself from the scene and do nothing more than observe, just like an outsider would.

The next step I take is to breathe. Naturally, this is important. We can't live without breathing, right? I'm pretty sure it would be hard to swim with a cow without taking a breath a time or two, as well. Breathing serves an important function here, which is to keep a person present in the moment. Think about it. You can't breathe in the past, and you certainly can't breathe in the future. You can only breathe in the present. When you do, it takes you out of the panic mode where you cannot think clearly, if at all.

The C stands for Center. When you stop and breathe, you can calm down and become centered. It's an amazing feeling—when you're centered, you can actually feel yourself connected to the earth, your feet squarely on the ground. You lose that sense of spiraling out of control and the desire to scramble and run around in circles so you can focus on the matter at hand. In my case, that was survival—for both me and the cow.

The last step is I, which stands for Inventory. Take an inventory of the resources you have available to you at the moment. In my case, those resources were water, or more aptly stated, the momentum of the water. The next thing I had was fear. While some people may not consider fear to be a resource, but instead a detriment, fear has a purpose. Fear fuels energy. All I had to was convert that energy into action. The next resource I had was a cow. I know I'm a minority with that one—not too many people have a cow as part of their inventoried arsenal in a time of crisis.

The next time you have a WTF day, use SBCI and see how much difference it makes in your outcome. You have resources—thankfully, and they are probably better than a cow, a rushing river, and a panic attack. There are friends, books and information, technology, time, money, and experiences on your side. Inventory what is available to you. When you do, what originally looks bleak and like a lost cause transforms itself into a workable situation. You can devise a plan to produce a different outcome than the one your imagination conjured, which is usually the worst-case scenario.

It's amazing how much difference it makes to stop, breathe, center, and inventory when life throws us challenges. Suddenly, you see things from a different, far better, perspective and your WTF transforms into OMG. Oh my God, look what I did! Look what I can do! I never thought I'd be capable of towing a cow across a swollen, angry river; but then again, I never thought a cow would be capable of towing me across one, either.

Today, I can find humor in that situation, and I can literally laugh out loud as I recant the story. When I was five, I would have done anything, *anything*, not to have experienced such a harrowing incident. But today, knowing that I survived it and the lesson it taught me, I wouldn't trade the experience for anything. Because I swam with a cow, I have redefined the WTFs in my life. They are no longer shocking or scary. When I stop, breathe, center, and inventory, I can transform any WTF into "Wow, Tequila Friday!"

And I have a cow to thank for that.

Who do you have to thank for the transformational experiences in your life—those that mold you into a stronger, more grateful, and happier person? They're there … practice a little SBCI and you'll find them.

\*\*\*

*Neary's experience is one that is incomprehensible to most. Most of all, it is inspiring to hear how she was able to overcome such an incredible challenge at such a young age, especially since the only resource she had was the hair at the rear end of a cow. For her, it was life saving.*

*Read on and hear about how someone older and with a very different background had to learn how to become resourceful just as quickly. As an astronaut on a major mission, his WTF to OMG moment was life changing.*

## THE WALK THAT ALMOST WASN'T

### Scott Parazynski

I have had multiple WTF moments, some which had the capability of impacting my career and others which could have affected my life. There was one, though, that had the potential to change the trajectory of my life and career. Naturally, it left a lasting imprint on me.

As an astronaut, a spacewalk was the dream of my life. I had trained extensively for this. I had envisioned it, and I finally was given the opportunity to really experience it. On my very first spacewalk, within 30 seconds of being outside the hatch, my tether froze and would not retract. If the malfunction wasn't corrected, and quickly, there would be no choice but to abort the walk.

Within only 15 minutes of fulfilling my dream, it appeared to be over before it started.

Initially, I was overcome with terror. The consequences if we couldn't find a safe and effective solution very quickly would be devastating. I would lose the opportunity of a lifetime to walk in space, and I knew it wasn't likely that I would get the chance to do it again. To me, it was a career limiting, or even career ending mishap.

One of the thoughts that ran through my mind was whether I had done something wrong. Yes, I scrambled to determine if I had inadvertently or mistakenly caused this to happen.

I had trained for malfunctions in the past, first as a doctor and later as an astronaut. I knew I had to transition quickly from fear into troubleshooting mode, so I had to slow down, review my options, and find a solution.

We didn't have the benefit of taking time to assess what had gone wrong or why. Finding a solution was our priority. After brainstorming the options, we improvised and found a way to compromise for the faulty equipment. In the end, they came up with a fix, using a couple tethers, like a mountaineer or an ice climber. We wrapped it up as tightly as possible and put it in the airlock. Then we used the two waist tethers, clipping one into a handrail, then clipping the other into the next handrail, and so on.

To my delight, my first spacewalk was a great success, even though it almost never happened.

Why had the tether malfunctioned? I later learned that a technician had used the wrong lubricant, which froze the tether. Sometimes things can go wrong, and they aren't always within our control. Regardless of the reasons, it is the solution that must be our highest priority.

That kind of resourcefulness requires a mental transformation. I knew that the fear of failure and embarrassments were not constructive emotions at that point. But those emotions were quite real. After all, this malfunction affected many more people than me; there were a lot of people observing and waiting. It was the first joint United States-Russian spacewalk, and we were docked to the Russian space station. It was a mission that required international collaboration, so, yes, it was a big deal.

Obviously, we had to figure out the mechanical solutions and then determine any out-of-the-box ideas that might work. In consultation with mission control, I was given permission to complete the walk with the solutions at hand.

It was, indeed, a lesson in resourcefulness. Rather than panicking because the world was watching, I had to dip deep into trusting myself. After this experience, I have learned that the time between shock and awe to constructive innovation and problem solving is much shorter now.

OMG! This awareness has been transformative. I carry these lessons into my personal and professional life. As an entrepreneur, I face problems all the time, as I know many do. Some are predictable; others are unforeseen. Regardless, I have been able to leverage that same extreme focus in everything I do.

This experience strengthened my ability to tune out the extraneous and focus on the problems at hand. Also, it enabled me to coach the teams around me to do the same. The NASA example is a wonderful model for the highest functioning teams. When that is leveraged with the collective experiences of the whole team, you can invariably come up with constructive solutions to the challenges you face.

One aspect of my medical and astronaut training that underpins my experience is that I've learned not to be satisfied with superficial knowledge, but rather to go deeper. I learned the need to understand how things are supposed to work, how they might fail, and then the need to have a plan B, C, and D should they fail, and when they fail. No one is smart enough to think about all of the potential problems that could happen; therefore, you need the depth of experience and a team around you to brainstorm a solution.

I'm now able to compress the timeline from WTF to OMG! NASA's repeated ability to take situations that are nearly impossible, or seemingly so, and then finding brilliant solutions has enabled me to become part of a larger-than-life mission.

Every challenging life experience I have had since then has benefitted from the experience gained in that spacewalk. The same mindset and mental preparation benefitted me when I was experiencing excruciating back pain while climbing Mt. Everest and was faced with trying to figure out how I to descend safely. I learned to be resolute and get the job done as safely as possible. My life depended on it.

There are so many correlations between a space flight, mountaineering, and life. Yes, the lessons learned while walking in space can transfer to mountain climbing … or in facing the many challenges and obstacles that life can bring.

I know now that whatever I face, I've done it before, and I can do it again. I remind myself that I can do this! To quote our famous flight director, Gene Kranz, failure is not an option. Giving up is not an option, either. That, perhaps, is the greatest lesson I received from my WTF moment … and one I am grateful for — even though I couldn't see it at the time.

*** 

*Most of us won't ever navigate ourselves through space, but I think most of us can relate to unexpected problems or misfortunes that have the potential to be life altering and require immediate attention. While under a great deal of pressure, Scott was fortunately able to shift his thinking so he could troubleshoot and find the solution to his WTF moment. Our next author didn't navigate through space, but she did make an incredible navigate through tragedy. Let's hear what she has to say.*

## NAVIGATING A NEW COURSE

### Annie Evans

I have had many WTF to OMG moments, but the first and most complete was when the boat I had logged 44,000 sea miles on got lost at sea with all souls on board lost. Obviously, I wasn't there.

When I got the news, I thought my life was over… I loved that boat, and all of my history and belongings were with it. But most important, my life-partner for all those years, who I still loved, was among those lost. I didn't know some of the others who were more recent crew members that were picked up when the original crew left and/or didn't make it back to boat for whatever reason, including the captain's son, my stepson, and other key personnel.

I was so devastated, and I still have bouts with survivor's guilt. As the celestial navigator (there was no GPS in those days) and honestly I was one of the main forces of keeping things together, I felt I had abandoned them. I left, because I had had to be a force of keeping things together. My mate had too much of a lackadaisical attitude and took to drinking too much wine.

While that was allowed for others from guests to crew, there were a few scary moments, and I just needed to take a break. I meant to go back, but I never did.

It was a beautiful comfortable boat, handmade and very fast – too fast for its original design. It had spent much time in various boatyards undergoing repairs and strengthening.

My "husband" and owner of the boat was a retired (medical) airline pilot, so the fact that there was such a relaxed attitude was alarming, and it was getting worse, which is why I left. He shouldn't have been so out of tune with the dangers we faced on an ongoing basis.

What I learned during those years was several graduate degrees of education with my highest degree being in problem solving. I also had to learn how to put fear aside and go to sleep, even in raging storms that put the boat and crew in incredible danger at times.

We only had an outboard motor fitted to the catamaran, which was only for getting in and out of harbors or very short bits – so we had to rely on the wind and sails. Further, we could only carry so much gasoline, so quite often we had no motor. We also had limited battery power; we had a ham radio that did work much of the time, but no battery power – no radio.

There were a couple instances when I thought all was going to be lost. One was when we were sailing back to California and about 1,500 miles away from land when the shackle holding both shrouds of the main mast broke, and the mast was flopping like a rubber tube. If the mast was lost, we would have been done for – although I am picturing even now how we could have hopefully somehow limped back to land. We had a good crew at the time, and we got the huge sails down. With the mast still flopping back and forth like a very limp d**k, a most precious friend (RIP) climbed the ~60' mast and was able to string a new shroud from the masthead. With the mast now jerry rigged, we were able to make it to California.

In fact, in the last three days of getting to San Francisco, we averaged over 300 miles per day, which is normally unheard of on a boat like ours.

There are amazing stories that I can tell ... from pulling ourselves off the rocks to many life-or-death moments. But I loved all the adventure, and if I had been lost, I wouldn't have regretted it – there were just such incredible things I got to see. The life was just incomparable, despite the hardships.

The islands, the people, the sea life – it all filled my heart, and to this day, I can still go back to distinct memories of the most beautiful spiritual moments.

I also went on to live an adventurous life, traveling and working in many countries.

OMG:

If took me a long time to get to the OMG—as I said, I thought my life was over when she was lost. I didn't know how to start over, for a while I didn't want to.

Finally, I realized I was young and my whole life was ahead of me. I was a seasoned problem solver and productive being. My entire life was rolled into such incredible experiences, and I was adept at learning new skills and being the consummate problem solver and idea creator. I went on to do really amazing things and have had a full life in senior corporate management. In addition, I became an entrepreneur (at first on the side, but now it is my life).

My departure from corporate by a new CEO was sudden and rude. I had been one of the main pillars to stake a start up from $4 million to $26+ million a year as one of the creators. Eventually, I became the Supply Chain Director in charge of sourcing, purchasing, production, quality and international logistics. We purchased materials all over the world and shipped through all the various hurdles of the times to get on time delivery and supply the product for sales to reach an impressive level.

I produced product in more than eight countries and was able to create and maintain fast loyalty from my suppliers—many remain friends to this day. I am extremely proud of my work product throughout my life.

Yet, I had a troubled past and rarely shared my story with others, although I did often help others overcome their problems on a limited basis … but there were parts of my life that even my family didn't know.

I finally told my story to my good friend, Ryan Long, as he had told me his troubled past. He kept leaning back further and further, and when I finally ended my story, he said, "Annie, you have to tell your story. You can help so many people." I immediately said, "No, Ryan, I do not tell my story."

Driving home that night, I realized that I always wanted to write about my adventures, and it suddenly dawned on me – what was I thinking? Was I just going to tell all the good parts of my life? I knew I had helped others along the way…

Suddenly, my OMG came to me! One of my purposes in life was to help others find their purpose and passion and how they can navigate their own course in life. They don't have to settle on things that don't suit them – everyone should constantly work on their goals and dreams, and they need to really work to believe that all is possible. If we really are doing what inspires us, things will come easier. That applies to every aspect of our lives – from who our friends are, who we marry, and how we contribute and grow.

I believe in doing the work. Many have told me that people don't want to hear that as they advise me on marketing and related things – but the truth is we all have to work on ourselves. We can obtain our goals and dreams, but they don't just fall into our lives. We need to set goals and reevaluate them all the time – things change. Many things are out of our control, and sometimes we really need to make adjustments, but I am always looking to be happy … and that takes work, as well.

*** 

*Annie's story reminds us that sometimes things happen for a reason. In no way are we minimizing the tragic loss of life, for that will always have a deep and lasting impact on those who survive. Instead, her story serves to remind us that even during times of grief, those left behind have a purpose. The OMG moment here is in the realization that Annie's WTF experiences likely kept her from being one of the victims who lost their life in that accident, and being able to discover new, challenging, and enriching opportunities that enabled her to grow and make a positive, lasting impact on others' lives. Annie was given a chance to begin anew, both personally and professionally, and in the process, she found that it was possible to rediscover happiness without regret. That's something worth working for, isn't it?*

# AN INTROVERTED KEYNOTE SPEAKER

## Ruben Gonzalez

About a month before competing in the Salt Lake City Olympics, something happened that changed my life. A fifth-grade kid from my neighborhood came up to me and said, "Hey, Ruben, when you get back from the Olympics, will you be my show-and-tell project at school?"

I told him, "Sure, sounds like fun." I only agreed because I thought every kid must be showing something that day, so I'd be in and out of there in five minutes. Then my competitive side came out. I thought, I'm going to win show-and-tell. I'll finally get my gold medal. I'll take my luge sled, my helmet, and my Olympic Torch (I had been a torchbearer). No prisoners.

**WTF Moment**

After the Olympics, I went to his school, assuming that I would be speaking to a classroom of twenty-five to thirty students. Instead, the principal walked me into the school's gymnasium, which was filled with over two hundred kids—the entire fifth grade class was assembled. Show-and-tell for a classroom of kids had, somehow, turned into an assembly.

The principal said, "Have at em. You have 45 minutes."

I was terrified. I'd never even taken a speech class because I'm such an introvert. Right then, the exit door looked so inviting. Then I said a prayer, "God, what do I do now?!" What I felt I needed to do was to tell them my story and give them some tips on how they can achieve their goals and dreams.

And then, something amazing happened: As I told the kids all of my Olympic stories, all the knowledge I had picked up from a lifetime of being a student of success started pouring out of me. Half the time, I didn't know what the next thing out of my mouth would be. I just put it on autopilot and poured my heart out to them.

These kids heard forty-five minutes of funny Olympic stories illustrating the principles of success they would need to follow in order to succeed in life. After the talk, as I was packing my things, a group of teachers encircled me; a posse, of sorts, surrounded me. Each face had a look of astonishment, and they said, "What do we have to do to get you to stick around for another hour? If you'll stay another hour, we'll pull the fourth graders out of class. They need to hear your story!"

I told my posse, "Hey, that was kind of fun, bring 'em on!" In the end, my second speech was a little better than my first.

Afterward, the principal said, "Ruben, you have a gift. You're better than the speakers we pay. You need to do this for a living."

I asked him, "What? You get paid for show-and-tell?"

"No, it's the speaking profession!"

Well, I thought about it. Sharing my stories with those kids was a blast. I was being 100 percent myself. It felt effortless. And the teachers said my story was impacting the kids in a very positive way.

Everyone has a unique ability or area of brilliance: a gift, a talent that is so strong that is makes work seem effortless. Most of the time, it is something that seems so natural to us that we totally discount it.

That is why it is important to give a lot of weight to the compliments that others share with us, because other people can usually see our unique talents better than we can.

**OMG Moment**

Totally by chance, I had stumbled onto doing something that used my greatest talent: connecting with other people to inspire and equip them to be their best.

For three days, I thought about everything the teachers had said to me. They said I had a "gift." And, then, just like that, I quit my job. When I quit my job and started speaking professionally, my thinking was, "If I can sell a copier, I can sell myself as a professional speaker. I know I can make it happen and I will make it happen."

Since that day in March, 2002, I've spoken for more than 100 Fortune 500 companies in five continents, and my books have sold over 300,000 copies.

Thank God I didn't run out the door when I saw all those kids.

Thank God that, instead of running from my fear, I ran right into it. Facing my fear changed my life.

*\*\*\**

*What Ruben doesn't tell us is that he is a four-time Olympian, competing in the luge, undeniably one of the most dangerous of all Olympic sports. Ruben could race down an icy pipe at speeds up to 90 miles per hour, but momentarily froze in fear when faced with the prospect of talking to a couple hundred fifth graders. LOL. A simple "show and tell" led Ruben to a Gold Medal career. His story "shows" us that we can overcome our fears, and when we do, it can unlock gifts we didn't know we had. Now, that's quite telling, isn't it?*

## YOU CAN BUILD ANYTHING WITH FAITH

### Bill Way

As a little kid, I always knew that someday, somehow, I would be in business for myself. I had absolutely no idea how, or what. But I felt such certainty, passion and was just too naïve to question myself.

I had no money, trust fund, or help from anyone. As it turned out, I was not to have a college degree or even a completed high school education. You might already be asking yourself, WTF?

Having become bored with high school, I dropped out. With few skills, I really needed some direction and, of course, a good job. My first couple jobs had felt lacking in potential, such as lawn care and security guard. But then at the age of 19, I started working in the home construction field. I knew nothing about that, either, but my dad had taught me to work with basic tools. After he gave me a one-day "crash course" in home-building, I was able to "fake" my way into that job. The key was that I told them the one thing I did know better than most was "how to work" and offered to work FREE for the first week while they evaluated me.

Blown away by my sheer audacity and confidence, they gave me a chance. It was a great opportunity to learn carpentry and construction management on the job. Frankly, I worked so hard and showed so much interest that they put up with my lack of knowledge. And by the way, they did end up paying me.

While I was not seeing a path to building a business, I absolutely loved the industry and took a great deal of interest in it. I never imagined I could have so much fun while working so hard!

The father-son company I worked for noticed my passion and took me under their wing, teaching me everything they knew. They certainly didn't have to. In just a year, I knew everything they knew about building houses. Dave and Red had given me a great gift. I later learned successful people often do that when they observe such zeal.

Meanwhile, the developer they worked for had also noticed me. I knew they were expanding, and I saw this as an opportunity. Figuring that unless they knew I was interested, they probably would not think to ask me, I went to them and asked if I could build houses for them, also, just like my employer was doing. Everyone was talking about the great job I was doing, so they said yes.

I was given the opportunity to frame and enclose as many homes as I could. In one month!

The next morning, I woke up with the biggest WTF moment in my life.

What had I done? You see, there were a few problems. I had

never done this before, but more important, I didn't have the required tools. I didn't even have a crew. To make matters worse, I also didn't have any money, financing, and not even any credit. OMG! Anyone observing me at that time would have had to think I was way over my head, to say the least—maybe even a bit crazy.

How was I going to do this?

Despite the challenges before me, it never once occurred to me that I couldn't do it. I knew I was going to figure it all out. Somehow. And I believed there had to be a way to make it happen.

I didn't let panic or despair get to me for long. In a few short hours, it occurred to me that every time I had taken a leap, I had succeeded. Maybe that was because I was always saying to myself that "everything always works out for me." I started noticing that somewhere along the way, that started to become the truth. And I was beginning to learn one of the most important success principles of my life: I can find evidence to support whatever I "choose" to believe. My "self-talk" had been critical to that process. All that being the case, I choose my beliefs, thoughts, words, and actions very carefully.

I was determined to figure this out, and even more important, I was going to make it happen. OMG, I simply had to. Quitting was not an option.

I immediately went back into my usual way of thinking. Sure, I'd doubted myself, albeit momentarily, but I put myself back on the trajectory of success ... and for me, that trajectory has always been led by faith and belief, to the point of absolute certainty. Certainty is faith on steroids!

Since then, anytime I catch myself feeling WTF (and in this instance, the F could stand for fear), I turn to a more positive F word. That word is faith. Faith in myself and faith in a Higher Power has always been there for me. It helped me find my way and the way to actually build homes … starting without a crew, without a lot of experience, without any money, but with faith.

Did it happen? Oh, yes, it did. I was asked to build as many houses as I could. I proved to myself and to everyone else that I could do that, and to extremely high standards, I might add.

How many houses was I able to build? Four houses in one month, I kid you not. I proved myself and my abilities, and in doing so, earned a reputation for being someone who always delivers on my promises. Fifty houses in a single year. Hundreds in my building career.

This start morphed into a general contracting and land development career. The developer had so much confidence in me that he eventually offered to co-sign a multi-million-dollar line of credit—without me even asking. At the time, I had a net worth of less than $10,000, little money, and hardly any credit experience. WTF to OMG!

Since then, I did go back to college and furthered my education there and elsewhere. I've been able to do so much throughout the course of my career. But the greatest lesson I've learned throughout my life, and one that has been proven repeatedly, is that the Universe will always show me a way if I step out in faith.

It never fails. It is law.

Anything is possible as long as we hold onto faith and take just a little action. Faith has never failed me. And faith is simply a decision. Choose a worthy belief, look for evidence to prove it is true, have faith, and take action.

For over 50 years I've built business after business using the same principles. That wakeup call gave me the answers. Once I cleared my mind of anxiety and fear, I replaced that with audacity and action. Then I was able to figure out how to make it happen.

Looking back, I can only laugh when I recall that brief moment in time when I doubted myself. A long history of successes in life and business has shown me those doubts and second thoughts were nothing more than figments of my own imagination.

I always remind people that whenever they find themselves in a WTF moment, they should assume that there is a gift, an awakening, a transformation, or an ah-ha opportunity within it. It has always been that way for me, and it continues to be so. Now I take great joy in giving back by lifting up budding entrepreneurs in any way I can, just as my mentors did for me. I encourage you to reach out; see my contact information which can be found at the end of this book.

I'm Bill Way, and I'm proof that with faith, you can build anything if you simply believe and take just a little action. Please don't ever forget this.

\*\*\*

*Wow! It is so inspiring to see how Bill used his WTF moment to embark on and accomplish an unlikely career milestone. Even more inspiring is his unwavering faith that the Universe will find a way to make it happen. Read on and meet Adam, who was also pursuing a career in an industry he loved, and discover how his WTF moments guided him directly into the career he loves today.*

# BUILDING A CAREER…
# ONE WTF AT A TIME

### Adam Edelstein

I've known since age seven I wanted to be on the radio—specifically on a morning show, entertaining people who are getting ready for work or school … or perhaps as a professional hockey announcer. I certainly did not want to wear a suit and tie, like my father did, while doing some monotonous job that I didn't enjoy.

After graduating from college, I hosted morning shows on small radio stations in upstate New York, Michigan, and Pennsylvania, before landing in Worcester, Massachusetts. Each new gig took me to a larger market with slight pay increases that were still straddling the poverty line.

After working on the air in Worcester a little more than a year, I was offered a full-time job recruiting blood donors and managing blood drives for the American Red Cross in Central MA. That became my primary job, with benefits; however, they allowed me the flexibility to keep the morning radio show part-time. It was the best of both worlds. I was also hired by

Worcester's American Hockey League (AHL) team as the in-arena host during home games. Basically, I was the guy with the microphone, entertaining fans with promotions in the stands during breaks in play and on the ice between periods. I had fulfilled my dreams of becoming a morning radio personality and working for a professional hockey team, and they were what I call my paid hobbies. The "real" job was flexible, social, paid the bills, and provided decent health insurance. After 12 years working for the Red Cross, more than doubling the blood collections in my territory, I needed a change.

A co-worker at our cluster of radio stations had been diagnosed with Type 1 diabetes and joined the steering committee for the American Diabetes Association (ADA) fundraising walk in Central Massachusetts. He got our three radio stations involved by promoting the walk, and I was asked to emcee the event.

It turns out the ADA Walk Manager was in the process of being promoted, and they were looking for someone to take over the Central Mass event. It was another flexible position that would allow me to continue my first love of being a morning radio announcer. At that time, I was hosting the morning show on a country music station, while, at the same time, doing the news and cohosting on a rock station in the studio next door and providing newscasts for our hot adult contemporary station, which can be heard into Boston.

After four years of building that Diabetes Walk from a $90,000 a year event to a $250,000 event, the ADA decided to reduce events and combine the Central MA and Boston walks, eliminating my position. I knew I'd be out of a job within 6 to 8 months and started putting out feelers, though I no longer wanted to work in fundraising. It's essentially a sales position with financial goals, which I find very stressful. I enjoyed the event management part, meeting people who are affected by diabetes and providing information and resources to help them; however, the pressure to collect more and more money became overwhelmingly stressful.

Again, I found myself in need of a job to pay the bills, but that would also allow the flexibility to start at 10 a.m. I wasn't willing to give up morning radio or working hockey games. But wait, there's more—by then, I had also added stand-up comedian to my resume, performing locally on occasion.

WTF. Professionally, I felt the walls closing in and didn't know how it would work itself out a second time. I became extremely depressed and destitute. I was in a very dark place, and it was affecting my thoughts and behaviors. My wife became concerned. I felt that the only thing that could dig me out of the hole was a job.

OMG. Out of the blue, I received a call from the co-chair of the Diabetes Walk Committee, who had become a friend over the course of the past four years we'd spent working together on the event. She asked if I knew anyone who might be interested in working at the medical school as a grant writer. I said, "How about me?" She was surprised I was looking, and I filled her in. She said I was overqualified for that job; however, the Diabetes Center of Excellence at the medical school needed someone to create and manage a website describing their diabetes research and care, build them a social media presence, manage special events on campus, and other such duties. She knew I had no intentions of leaving the radio station and essentially created a position for me. She convinced her directors that I would be a perfect fit.

One of the events I manage is an annual Diabetes Day on campus that brings together the scientists and staff from the research labs and care teams from the clinic to share information and successes on both sides. They also give Employee Excellence Awards for science and care team members. I had attended the first annual event as an invited guest while working for the ADA. I helped organize the second annual during my first year working at the Diabetes Center of Excellence. The third annual became my responsibility. While I thought I had checked each box and handled every detail, during the awards presentations, they surprised me with a You Make a Difference Award, a peer-nominated award presented to employees who have contributed to the success of the Diabetes Center of Excellence. LOL.

***

*Being knocked down and seeking employment through no fault of his own, Adam was sucked into the what the hell, what am I going to do hole of despair, not once, but twice. Each time, though, the door that closed surprisingly led him to a door that opened into a position that suited him well and provided better income, benefits, and opportunities. OMG! Did these positions that fulfilled him and enabled him to continue to enjoy his passions just fall into his lap? Or did the universe coordinate the chain of events in order to directly led Adam to progressively rewarding roles that ultimately awarded him for his contribution? Hindsight provides insight—you be the judge.*

# A CALL TO SERVICE

## Eric Power

I was proud to serve my country for ten years from 2002 to 2012. During that time, I had several deployments overseas and was injured a few times.

When I left the service in 2012, I returned to civil life in the United States. Due to my disabilities, I tried to get my VA disability but found the process to be frustrating at best. I wasn't successful, but I wasn't sure why, even though I was doing everything I was told. I looked for answers anywhere I could, but even with the assistance of attorneys, I wasn't making any progress and wasn't receiving my benefits.

Without answers, I stopped trying. Instead, I read everything I could about the benefits, the law, and what it took to be successful. After several months, I applied again, this time on my own, without any assistance.

The good news was that I was successful. My first try applying for benefits solo resulted in receiving 90 percent of my benefits, which is rare, almost unheard of. After following up and applying again, though, I received 100 percent of the benefits I was entitled to.

The significance of this is that veterans across the country face this same issue. Like me, they have earned their benefits, and they deserve them, especially when their service results in short- or long-term disabilities. These benefits are critical to their wellbeing and their ability to overcome the obstacles and challenges they will face in their future.

Now, at the time, I was going to business school. In a marketing class, we were told if we could solve a problem, we could have a business. They even asked us to come up with a fictitious company name and create a Facebook page and turn the leads in.

In the back of my mind, I wondered if I could help other veterans get their benefits, too. Grasping at straws, I created a fictitious business that promised to do that. Then I created the Facebook page and waited, although I didn't place much hope that this business idea would actually catch anyone's interest and build any steam.

In the end, I got approximately 50 leads. Thinking I was going to be in the low end of the group, I was surprised to find that I had the most leads in the class, with some only having one or two.

That's when my instructor told me that I should really turn this veterans disability assistance idea into a real business.

What? Me? Start a business? I didn't know how to start a business. I didn't know how to run a business.

But a part of me was thinking, why not? If not me, then who?

Suddenly, it occurred to me that I could actually turn this into a bonafide business. OMG! In my spare time, I started calling those 49 or 50 leads, and the next thing I knew I had clients. Within 6 months, I was making as much as I was making in my corporate job. In less than a year, I decided to quit my full-time job and go all in.

In 2015, I opened that business with only one employee—me. On my own, I picked up the calls and met individually with veterans to help them complete their applications for disability. After being successful and helping fellow veterans get their due benefits, my company grew. Today, we have 36 employees in house and 20 agents working from home. And it all started because I had a WTF moment.

WTF, I became disabled while serving my country.

WTF, I couldn't get the benefits that I had earned and deserved.

WTF, I didn't know how to start or run a business.

But OMG, once I figured out how to receive those benefits, I could turn it into a business that provided for me and my family. OMG, I've been able to help others get their due benefits, while helping others through philanthropy. I'm very proud that I have been able to redirect and utilize some of the revenue that I've been able to generate to help others.

But the WTFs and OMGs don't stop there.

WTF, how was it that I, who had no business background, was awarded a star on the Walk of Fame in Las Vegas near my good friend, Frank Shankwitz, who cofounded the Make a Wish Foundation? OMG, what an honor!

I always look forward to finding the OMGs in my WTFs, and I won't ever stop searching for them, no matter what the situation. And I will always advise the young people who come under my mentorship and in my company to do the same.

\*\*\*

*I've known Eric Power for years, and we've become good friends during that time. Not only do I admire him for his service to our country, but I commend him for using his skills and talents to help others who have served. It is a WTF to OMG story that is honorable, and I thank him for his service to our country and his fellow veterans.*

# CONDOMS AND TEDDY BEARS

## Kerry Jacobson

I was in my junior year of high school when our town was hit with a financial shortfall and its budget was drastically cut. There was no money for anything. Public works was cut completely, and the schools had to operate on a shoestring budget that left them with no money to purchase textbooks or fund extracurricular activities, including sports. That year, there would be no track meets, baseball or basketball games, or Friday night football. The high school experience had been stripped to bare bones, leaving nothing but academics taught tired, old textbooks.

I was a good student and an athlete, and this didn't bode well with me. Everything I liked about school had been taken away, and that simply wasn't fair. After all, it wasn't our fault that the town didn't have any money. Yes, I felt the students were being punished. Sure, I complained, but then I realized that complaining wasn't going to change anything. If I didn't like it, there was something I could do. I could go to another school, one where I could play sports and have access to the resources I would need to complete my high school career and prepare me for my future.

The only other school in our area was a local Catholic boys' school, and because it was expensive, it wasn't an option for me, either. At the time, my parents were suffering financially, too. My father was a Baptist minister, and our family was poor. And while I was working three part-time jobs, I knew I couldn't afford to pay the high tuition for a private school.

In one of those jobs, I was a stockboy at a privately-owned drugstore. Let me set the scene. Back then, some products were not displayed in the aisles, but were discreetly and purposely not exposed to the customers. Condoms were one of them. We kept the condoms on a back wall, where they were out of reach (and seeing distance) of the shoppers, and if someone wanted to buy any, they had to ask the pharmacist for them. As you can imagine, the process could be quite intimidating, and for kids in high school, embarrassing.

At this time, safe sex was being heavily promoted by the medical community, as well as condom manufacturers. To create awareness of their products, the manufacturers started a promotional campaign, giving away single-pack condoms in an effort to entice users to purchase their product over the competition's. The sales representatives would deliver hundreds of condoms to us at a time, and the pharmacists were encouraged to give them away. The pharmacists, however, might have felt uncomfortable doing that, because we ended up with a box containing thousands of brand new single-pack condoms that were doing nothing but taking up space and gathering dust.

That's when I came up with an idea: what if I took the condoms to school and sold them? That would be the answer to my problems! With permission from my employer, I started my fourth job as a condom salesman. Between classes, I'd go to the locker room and sell a condom to my fellow classmates for one dollar a piece. Not only did I make enough money to pay for my tuition, but I made a couple thousand extra dollars. In addition, it also helped the drugstore get rid of the surplus stock … and even though I was a new transfer student at a Catholic school, I became rather popular. Yes, everyone got to know the condom guy.

I didn't know anything about being a salesperson or running a small business, but my little locker room side job paid off. I like to think that my ingenuity played a part in my success. While stripping a town's budget down to the bare bones was undoubtedly a last resort, everyone did the best they could at the time. Because I wanted to do the best that I could, as well, this presented me with an opportunity to find a solution. The fact that it was a win-win for me, my employer, and my classmates, well, let me just say, "OMG."

I wasn't the only person in my family who discovered a talent and entrepreneurial spark during this time of financial hardship. My mother also tapped into her creativity to add to the family's income. Mom was a seamstress, and she used to work in a nursing home. To make ends meet, she sewed homemade teddy bears and sold them to the nurses and staff for $10 each, earning $250 in her side business.

It was until later that I truly recognized the value in the experience and what it had taught me. Sometimes, the OMGs don't fully hit us until we gain some wisdom, experience, and, might I add, a touch of hindsight.

Initially, I had a WTF moment, thinking how unfair it was that I wouldn't be able to enjoy playing sports in school. Why was every other kid able to go to the school they wanted and participate in the programs they wanted, but not me?

Had it not been for that situation, though, I wouldn't have had an OMG moment, which was that I discovered that I had the ability to figure things out and come up with a solution. If it hadn't been for the budget cuts, I might not have ever known that problems are really opportunities to create solutions.

Many years later, as I create an enterprise that is inarguably the largest in the world of its type, I think back to that time when that gift was given to me. Who knows, without my WTF moment, I might not have ever sparked the entrepreneur within me, and many people might not have been able to avail themselves of my marketing talents.

Because I was the condom guy, I know that when I take the opportunity to step back and think about a situation, there is usually a solution.

There is an opportunity within whatever you are confronted with, and that is the greatest lesson I took away from my teenage experience. That opportunity is the gift that is embedded in the lesson, and that gift is of equal or greater magnitude than the pain that I experienced when financial struggles impacted my school.

In hindsight, I wouldn't trade that pain for the alternative, because I know that without it, I wouldn't have gained so much. The spark of entrepreneurism wouldn't have been lit, and my life likely would have taken an entirely different trajectory.

Everyone has WTF moments. Some believe that the world is conspiring to hurt them, and they feel helpless to counter it. They exclaim, "WTF!" or, perhaps, it is better spoken with a question mark, "WTF?" That's because they know *what* happened, but they're at a loss to understand *why* it happened.

There are some, though, who believe that when WTF moments occur, the universe is conspiring to help them. It's working to point them in a different direction or shift them into a different way of thinking. It's the universe's way of teaching us something we really need to know.

I propose, however, that both perspectives are true. If you think the world is conspiring against you, you are right. If you believe it is conspiring positively for you, you're also right. Whatever you believe will be your reality, and you will be able to will it the way you perceive it.

Thankfully, my reality was that the world was conspiring to help me. It was pushing me, forcing me to come up with a solution to a problem that I could have bemoaned and grudgingly accepted. I know I could have done what the majority of the students did and continued with the status quo, attending the same school, and complaining about the hand that fate dealt us. But I truly believe I was called to discover my potential and make a change in my life, and left to my own devices, I had to figure out a way to make that possible.

Hardships call for solutions. If it had not been for the economic hardships that our whole town all experienced, I wouldn't have figured out a way to pay my tuition and my mom wouldn't have found a way to earn some extra income. Neither of us would have ever dreamed of selling condoms or teddy bears.

I can say that I'm glad I did.

# WTF? I DIED!
# OMG! I DIED!

## Kristoffer Doura

My WTF? moment came about ten years ago when I collapsed on the football field at the Pittsburgh Steelers training facility. I was then placed into an ambulance and rushed to the hospital. I had no idea what was going on and was scared for my life.

When I arrived at the hospital, I was surrounded by 16 doctors, who diagnosed me. I was told it didn't look good. Not knowing what that meant, I was startled. All I could do was pray to God that I would survive and make it out of there.

I discovered that I was severely dehydrated, which had caused a blood clot in my leg. It was a life-or-death situation that required surgery to release the blood clot and the tension of that clot. I was told there wasn't enough blood flow or circulation pumping from my leg to my heart. I needed surgery, or my leg would have to be amputated in order to save my life.

I was sedated for the next steps of the process. Somehow, I went into a trance. For whatever reason, the energies kept me there unconsciously. Because of what I felt, I knew for a fact that it wasn't the end game.

While they were performing the surgery, I died. My heart stopped. It flatlined. I still get a tingle in my spine every single time I relive that moment.

I got a second chance in life. God had a purpose for me, which was another WTF moment. I made it! I'm still here, and I'm still breathing. I knew for a fact that my life wasn't over, because my purpose was bigger than who I was at that moment in time.

The discipline, the hard work, the consistency of what got me to the pros is the same tenacity I use in carrying out that purpose.

The surgery took 16 hours. When I woke up the next morning, seeing my family created an OMG! moment. Oh my God, I'm alive. Oh my God, I'm still breathing.

The doctors said I was truly blessed. They told me my heart failed because there wasn't enough oxygen, and my heart went through trauma. When I woke up that morning, I knew that I had to make a decision to hang up the cleats. My values lie with my family, and those values are more important to me than any professional sport.

Thankfully, I'm educated and have a master's degree in business. I realized that there was so much more for me to accomplish.

It took three months to get out of that hospital. I went in at 350 pounds and rolled out at about 280 pounds. There was a 70-pound loss of mass. What a big change, OMG!

When I decided to exit Pittsburgh, I returned to Miami, and it took about eight months to get back on my feet. I needed a wheelchair and crutches and had to rebuild myself from scratch. But I never quit. I knew when I became strong enough, I was going to put on a blazer and a smile and go after something bigger than me.

I became a financial adviser and have been doing this for seven years. Who would have thought?! What I'm doing today as a strategic adviser is bigger and more impactful than anything I've ever done. I've realized being a financial adviser, helping nonprofits with their legacies and how to be sustainable is an area of my expertise.

This is the reason, the OMG, I became a published author—to be able to make an impact and leave a legacy behind of helping others, becoming philanthropic, spending time in my community, and teaching others that when life throws you curveballs, they can bounce back. I did.

By becoming a financial adviser, I've been able to consult nonprofit organizations and business owners, helping them to take a WTF moment and learn from those experiences, understand how to overcome those challenges, and transition to an OMG moment.

My OMG moment is making a big impact today, and I feel it allows me to put good into the world. I help people identify how they can also impact and touch others, help people in need, and feed children. I'm living my OMG moment. I'm in total awe to know that what I'm doing today will impact many lives tomorrow.

I'm excited and blessed. I know I have so much more resilience because of my WTF moment. For that reason, I wouldn't change a thing from the second I dropped on the field to today. It brought me to where I am today, and it blessed and enriched my life. Without it, I wouldn't be here making an impact through my story and my legacy.

I love what I do. I'm inspired and excited. I'm a philanthropist, an author, an actor, and a gentle giant. That's what's important.

WTF? It really happened!

OMG! God is great!

\*\*\*

*What a remarkable transformation and what an incredibly positive message! Kristoffer's WTF moment could have been detrimental, but he found the gift it brought to him—the blessing to do something he loves, while making a memorable impact on those he serves and meets. While he calls himself a gentle giant, I know that the biggest part of him is his heart—the very heart that stopped beating, but came back to life with a renewed purpose. OMG, we are glad it did!*

## FOR THE LOVE OF NICK

### Kari Petruch

My oldest son was born in 1988. He was a beautiful normal baby boy, and I loved him so much! Then seven months later, I found myself pregnant with my daughter. WTF? I was not prepared for two children 15 months apart. Having two so close in age was definitely like having twins. When Katy was 6 months old, I noticed that she was not progressing in the same way that her brother did. I told her doctor that something was not quite right. The doctor told me not to worry, she was perfectly fine. At one year, I took her to the doctor again. I asked him if her hearing was okay. He told me that she was fine and that she was depending on her older brother for communication.

When Katy turned two, I insisted the audiologist test her for hearing loss. I absolutely knew that she was not hearing the way that she should. The audiologist opened the door of the hearing booth and had a sadness on her face that left an imprint I will never forget. She told me that my daughter was deaf. WTF? I cried big tears for about a week. I then moved in the direction of helping her to communicate in the best way possible with every possible tool that I could get. I was then pregnant with my third child. I was terrified about having a deaf child and wondered if I could live up to the responsibility of being the best mom I could be. My childhood was not good, and I was scared out of my mind.

My daughter's story is her own, but this is a story about my third child, Nick.

The pregnancy of my third child had been full of some incredible stresses. I lost so much weight with this pregnancy. The complications were many. One month before my due date, baby Nicholas decided to enter the world as a 9-pound premature baby. He was a sweet baby that slept 7 hours at night when he came home. He was so amazing! At about 15 months, I started noticing things that weren't quite right. He seemed to have no fear, and I wasn't sure he was hearing everything I said to him. Because of my daughter, I knew that he was hearing some things, and I considered what the doctor said about siblings talking for each other.

I watched him very closely. He was my little daredevil. At 18 months old, his father received orders to go to Korea. Two days before his dad was to leave, I was tying my daughter's shoes when Nick started to jump off the couch. My arm instinctively flung out and pushed him down on the couch. Moments later, his brother came in to ask me a question while I was still tying those shoes, and Nick jumped. The only thing that hit that table were his top three teeth. There are still pictures out there somewhere of my poor darling child's mouth. What I found incredible was that after the initial pain of the impact, my sweet baby never fussed or complained about the pain. As a mother, that was a little frightening. Babies are not that brave. WTF?

The daredevil adventures continued, and Nick had to be watched closely. He would do crazy things one day, and the next day he would decide that mommy needed lotion on her legs. I was so confused. Who was this little guy? We enrolled him in a little preschool program that was just one morning a week. I got the call. "Ummm, we think that Nick has a hearing problem." I had my strong suspicions already, and due to my experience with my daughter, I was a little more prepared this time.

I took my son for the hearing tests and knew the drill. He was Hard of Hearing. He received his first hearing aids and proceeded to flush them down the toilet. Because of his sister, I had learned how to pin those aids at the back of his collar using embroidery floss and a safety pin. This little smart kid figured out how to undo that within hours. OMG! I learned right then and there that I would be spending a lifetime trying to outwit the smart kid. The hearing loss was something that I knew and could help with. What I was not prepared for was the adventures that were to come.

We had so many of these situations happen. He was doing flips off the diving board at three. He was riding a bicycle without training wheels by three. He was reading by the time he was three. He was a super little man with super intelligence and super strength. OMG! What in the world was I to do? How could I keep up with this child?

That was the daredevil stuff, and then there were other things that I found so different. Alarm bells went off in a strange way for me. I began to be concerned about his emotional development. One day, Nick was really enraged that a cat scratched him, and he started swinging the cat by its tail. I ran to help the cat and put Nick in his room so I wouldn't beat his butt. WTF? Who does that to a cat? I had never seen such a thing. Was my son devoid of any feeling for animals? OMG, what am I to do?

Soon after this incident, Nick decided it would be a good idea to try and ride on the back of our lab/retriever mix dog. Really? I made a rule that if our dog went into her kennel, Nick was not allowed to reach in or bother her. I had to continually smack his hand until he learned. Nick decided that putting his hand up to an open flame from a gas stove was also a good idea. Hand smacking again. There was no reasoning. He only learned not to do these dangerous things when I smacked his hand.

We were a military family. We moved quite a bit, and his father was not home very much. I had to figure this out. The one thing I knew was that I loved my son, and I believed that he would someday figure all of this out. So, Nick met the cutoff date for attending kindergarten. I was very concerned about his socialization skills, so I took him to a local mission Catholic school and asked the nuns if they would assess my son. Sister Mary went away with Nick, and when she came back, she asked Sister Joan to take Nick for a little while. She explained to me that Nick was not ready. He was far superior in intelligence but was behind socially by about two years. I was shocked and cried. She was so kind to me and told me, "Nick is a gifted child with incredible potential. School would be boring for him and would give him an excuse to create his own entertainment." She then suggested that he attend an all-day preschool so he could learn the social skills that he will need to attend kindergarten. She also suggested that he be involved in some sporting activity all year long. So, I decided to follow her direction.

Nick went to preschool and loved his teacher. He learned about social rules from a wonderfully patient woman. She was not a teenager but a woman who had raised her own children and was teaching these little ones because of her love for them. To let my child go was just another step in the right direction for Nick.

By the end of the year, Nick was deemed ready for kindergarten. Then the tests came. Nick had an extremely high IQ. OMG! The gifted programs were just beginning then. Let me tell you that if a child had a high IQ but had behavioral problems, then they were out. Because of my daughter and her needs, I was aware of the IEP (Individual Education Plan). My deaf daughter's plan was easy compared to Nick. Yes, he was hard of hearing and gifted, but there was more, and no one could figure out what that was. We were on a path that I never expected. What Nick needed was someone who believed in him, NO MATTER WHAT!

The school decided that the answer to helping this gifted child would be to send extra work home for him. Of course, at five years old, he did not want to do homework, and he was smart enough to figure out that the rest of the kids did not have this added work. He battled me. He said that it wasn't fair (a term that he learned from other children in school). What was I to do?

We made a game of it every day, and he was okay with that. Then, in the middle of kindergarten, he was uprooted to move to Korea. He couldn't read the signs and was very angry that he couldn't understand the language that was in front of him. He did make friends with the Korean children quickly, though, and as children do, they taught him Hangul.

The daredevil antics continued. Nick decided to jump from the top of a hill during a baseball game. Three days later, he was hopping on one foot. We took him to the emergency room. He had an incredible pain tolerance. When they asked him if he was in pain, he said, "Not really, I just can't walk on my foot." The X-rays came in, and Nick had a spiral fracture of his growth plate. The social worker and the police were called in. So, we learned later that this kind of injury was one that happens in child abuse. We tried to explain what happened, but there was no listening until … Nick came barreling down the emergency room hall on his crutches at the speed of a runner yelling, "Look, Dad, I can go really fast with these!" The entire staff looked at us. It was then that they understood that Nick was his own special kind of kid, and that we were doing the best we could. LOL!

During the summers, I devoted my time to my children with arts, crafts, cooking, and science experiments. Nick loved summers! This summer, he learned about all kinds of chemical reactions and memorized his multiplication tables. We started him in Hapkido school, and he was happy. He started first grade this way. Happy. He did magnificently in first grade, and we were so proud of Nick. The summer came and went, then he began second grade. My husband had received orders to move to Fort Bragg, North Carolina. We decided to let the children know that we were moving about two weeks before we moved.

We learned that this was a very bad idea insofar as Nick was concerned. The consequences were more than we expected. The very next day, Nick pushed a child who was in front of him in line in school. He didn't tell us why, and the school suspended him for three days. I figured out was that this was the only way he could express his anger toward the change. He loved his school and Hapkido. He loved his little Korean friends that he played Pokémon with. He loved his life there, and we were going to take that away from him. He returned to school for the last week and was such a sad little boy.

Then, we moved to Virginia. During our first nine months in Virginia, we lived in a very crowded townhouse complex. My children rode the bus to school. Facing the challenges of the special education of both my daughter and son in this environment was particularly challenging. I had learned about IDEA (Individuals with Disabilities Education Act) and had spent years educating other parents about the law. I was a parent advocate for other children and continued to volunteer my time to help all of the parents and children that I could.

I had a difficult time with the Fairfax school system, that wanted to send my children to a magnet school. I wanted them to be educated in the school where they lived. So, Katy decided that she wanted to be in a school with other deaf children, and I decided that she was old enough to make that decision. Nick was to stay in his neighborhood school.

Within days of starting school, Nick, who was only eight years old, said something that upset a child who was two years older than him. This child decided to punch my son in the stomach. I was there. I do not remember what Nick said, but I do remember thinking that my son had just learned a valuable lesson about being respectful. Not … Nick got on that bus and beat the ever living crap out of that kid. He broke his nose and blackened his eye. WTF?

Because the bus had already driven away, I didn't see this, but learned about it an hour later when I was called to pick up my child. He was a bundle of tears and was suspended from school for three more days. I would not punish him, though his father said that I should. In my mind, he did what he had to do to stand his ground against a bully.

Not too long after this, I was called into a special meeting. A parent was threatening to sue me and my husband I was mortified. "What did my son do?" The principal explained that my son had stuck out his tongue at a little girl, and the parents were upset at this sexual aggression toward their daughter. I laughed so hard I couldn't breathe. As you can imagine, no one else in that room thought that this was funny. I then asked my son what happened. He said that she stuck her tongue out at him and that he just did the same back to her. The whole thing was dropped. LOL!

About a month later, I received a phone call from his teacher, who explained to me that I needed to encourage my child to tell the truth. She said that there were two new students in the class and that they were from Korea. She stated that Nick was pretending to translate for them in the classroom and that he needed to be honest. Again, another belly laugh. Nick could indeed speak fluent Hangul and could translate for these two children. I replied, "Do you have any idea where we have lived for the last two years?" When she answered that she did not, I told her we had lived in Korea and she was mistaken—Nick very well could translate—and then … I hung up.

That was my last straw. I absolutely knew that I had to be the one person in my son's life who believed in him. I understood at that moment that he needed his mom to be his champion.

Soon after, that we moved into government quarters at Fort Belvoir. At nine years old, we decided that it might be better for Nick to attend the same school as his sister. That worked out fairly well for the next year. During that year, life was interesting. Nick decided to paint the bathroom ceiling with spitballs and made carvings out of bar soap. He was a handful, and I loved him. I was less concerned with those kinds of things than I was about his compassion and empathy for others. Since his sister was now attending middle school and riding a different bus, it was determined that he could attend the school right there on Fort Belvoir. His fourth-grade teacher was amazing. She was even teaching her students Latin to increase their vocabulary. Nick loved her and soaked up as much information as she could give. For the first time, he was charged and ready to learn. I began to see a light within Nick and watched him attach to his teacher. OMG! She challenged my child in every way and inspired him to want to know more. She even challenged him to read Harry Potter with a dictionary by his side, which he did.

Following the nuns' encouragement, I involved Nick in sports, and he loved it. We were at a practice and the coach said he was very upset with Nick for playing around in the outfield. I asked him why Nick was in the outfield—did he realize how fast Nick could pitch? The coach got angry and said that he didn't believe Nick had the attention span to stay focused on pitching. He told my son that if he could last an entire practice as a catcher that he could catch for the team. On that extremely hot day, my son lasted the entire practice as a catcher. OMG! His son, the pitcher for the team, cried at the end of the practice because his hand hurt from catching Nick's throws back to him. The coach stopped practice and put my son on the pitcher's mound to clock his pitch speed, which was 89 mph at 9 years old. The coach just stood there in shock. Again, I believed in my son even when no one else did. Nick pitched for many years to come. LOL!

During this time, my son met his best friend, Josh, whose mom asked me if my son had ever been diagnosed with Asperger's syndrome. I didn't even know what that was. At the time, his school was demanding that he be put on medication for ADHD, or they would not allow him to come back to school. I came back with a demand that he be tested by a psychiatrist that was not associated with the school system. I absolutely knew that kids who were hyperactive did not have the attention span to spend hours on anything. Because my child could spend hours reading a book and playing a game on the computer, this was illogical. My words to them were harsh. "You are not going to drug my kid. You are wrong." When the tests came back, the psychiatrist said, "If you had allowed that school to medicate your child, it could have done so much damage. Nick has Asperger's. What I would really like to know, is how in the world did you manage to raise such a well-adjusted child with Asperger's?" WTF! When the report was sent to Nick's school, I didn't receive an apology, however, from then on, their expectations from my baby changed. LOL!

There was a blizzard when Nick was 10, and he and his best friend, Josh, decided to make a little money by shoveling out the cars buried in the snow. These two amazing boys spent 12 hours shoveling snow and made about $1,000 together. Man, that was my kid. He was a worker and a good custodian of his money. Every dime he made went into a savings account.

Yet on another front, Nick has the propensity to get himself in trouble with other children. He would just say what he thought or tell the truth about what he saw. This was only accepted by his friend, Josh. Other children would take offense at his honesty. The things that he said to other children would provoke them and set their egos on fire. He was chased down many a time and even up a tree once. I had to consistently guide and reinforce the social norms with my precious son. There were many visits made to families so Nick to apologize for what he said to their children. There was much bridge building to do, and we worked on it constantly. It became routine for Nick to say, "I know … we gotta go apologize." One day, he hurt a sweet little girl's feelings. I tried to give him a warning look, but he didn't see me. However, he did see her face, and the tears that fell moved him to apologize. OMG! He was beginning to understand.

Because of instances like these, I constantly worried about his ability to care for others and whether he would awaken his compassion for others. There were people who told me he would not, but I couldn't accept that. Then something happened that eased my concerns. After having surgery, I was in a long leg cast, which prevented me from being able to chase after my son, who decided to play with his father's nunchucks in the living room. He didn't listen when I told him to stop, and the nunchucks flew out of his hands and broke a set of Murano glass that I cherished. To my surprise, I cried in response. Nick took one look at me, and for the first time, I saw his compassion for his mother. He came to me, and his remorse and compassion were immense. He cried for at least an hour. He didn't cry because he was in trouble. He cried because he made his mother cry. It was then that I knew that my baby would be okay. He did have compassion for someone that he loved. I thanked God for that revelation!

Because of his difficulty at school, Nick desperately wanted to be homeschooled, like his friend, Josh, but his father refused to agree to this. When he was 11 years old, Nick encountered his most difficult teacher. During an IEP meeting, this woman actually asked why she needed to face my son at all times when giving instruction. I answered, "Are you serious? Because he cannot hear you!" She was one tough teacher, and Nick became angry. She required her fifth-grade students to write a five-paragraph essay every week, which made my son so angry that he would have fits and sometimes even threw chairs. These children were not given writing prompts, and Nick was at a loss to figure out what to write about. Lucky Nick, his mom loved to write, and I structured Nick's writing prompts. He was able to turn in his outline, rough draft, and final draft every week with no chair throwing. LOL!

When Josh moved, Nick became incredibly sad, and for the first time, he cried about a friend. Josh was the first and only real friend my son would ever have during his school years and his heart was broken. So was mine. My son had developed an attachment to a wonderful friend, and he was taken away. I am moved to tears even today as I write about this. He cried, and I wept for him while he slept. My child was heartbroken, and I knew then that his heart was immense. You see, when all these people had given up on my wonderful child, I did not, and I wept for him and felt an incredible joy that he was able to bond with another child. Because of his older brother, I was acutely aware that these emotional strides happened much earlier for children. It was then that I moved my expectation of Nick's emotional development back a few years.

Nick recovered, and so did I. Life got a little easier for him, and he was able to find a place. Having that special friendship changed the way he interacted with other children. He stayed involved with sports and read a book a day. He really loved to read, and I supported him in this habit. He would tell me about all the things that he read about, and we would have discussions about the stories or what he learned about. His understanding of the world and the relationships between people grew. Just when he had built a happy place, his world was upset again when we moved to Germany. OMG! It wasn't as tough of a transition as we thought it would be. Nick adjusted so well. He really found a space there. He attended a K through 8th grade school and was expected to be responsible for the younger children, which he took that very seriously. He was such an example and was really beginning to catch up with his emotional development.

Just one year after we arrived in Germany, I had gastric bypass surgery. It was serious, and I was in the ICU for three days. His father decided that our children needed to visit me in the ICU, which was most traumatic for Nick. While he shed tears, hugged me, and told me he loved me, I could feel his pain and concern for me.

Very soon after that surgery, I got a job outside our home. Nick was doing well in school, and it was time for me to do something different. I spent my time running a deployment center for the Army. My son finally had stabilization and was able to develop friendships through school, sports and the very first robotics program. Nick also found a sweet girl to date. She was so lovely until she started talking to him about getting married one day. For Nick, that was like telling a 13 year old that she wanted to get married. Nick was not ready for commitment or even the thought of it. My darling son broke her heart. He ended that relationship in the way that his mother taught him—face to face he stood, and on the ground of integrity, he walked away. OMG!

During his senior year, Nick was really upset that he was not able to access the information that he needed from the Internet via the school, so he decided to lock up the computers in the school. WTF? It turned out that he crippled the entire school system throughout the Department of Defense Schools in Europe. When I picked him up from school, he very proudly told me what he had done. I turned the car around and took him straight to the principal's office. When I told the secretary that we needed to talk to the principal right now, she told me that the principal didn't have time and I would have to come back tomorrow. I very loudly said, "Let me guess. Your computers are locked up, and no one can access anything, and your staff cannot get to the mainframe to correct the problem." The principal heard me and came out immediately. Seeing the look on his face, Nick stared at the floor. It would be Nick's last act of defiance. The principal talked with Nick for about an hour, and then Nick went into the system and fixed the problem that he had created. He was permitted to remain in school but was no longer allowed access to the computers in the school. The fact that he was a model student since he was in the seventh age was his salvation.

Nick graduated from high school and became a magnificent person who has so much love and compassion for others. We never told Nick that he qualified for Mensa. We never told Nick that he couldn't have the relationship or life that he wanted. You see, I absolutely believed that if I believed in him, he would eventually awaken. Nick found his wife, Cat, and they fell in love. Much to our dismay. he married at the age of 20. Cat had three children from a previous marriage and was eight years older than him. By grace, she really understood how Nick processed information. Nick and Cat worked to achieve their goals together and were fantastic parents for her three children.

Then, our beautiful Noah was born. Noah was born with a rare disorder. He had to be fed every hour or hour and a half and had to be constantly watched for the first two years of his life. Again, WTF? The two of them learned to be a team and took care of that baby. Noah is doing beautifully today.

After working for a company for six years, Nick wanted to take a chance for a position with another company. When he called me, the words that rang true were, "Baby, nobody cares about those requirements. Get the interview and show them what you can do." Tesla hired him immediately after the interview. OMG!

Just seven months after their fifth child was born, Cat's newborn niece was being taken away from her mother. Cat and Nick took this beautiful, drug addicted baby into their home. Because? She is family. OMG!

This wonderful man that so many gave up on is an incredible father and husband. I am grateful to God every single day for the grace and blessing of my son! So, WTF (How do I help my son?), OMG (He has become an amazing man!) and LOL (You were all wrong!)

*\*\**

*Kari reminds us that our WTF moments might not be moments, but days, weeks, months, and even years. While they can be extremely trying, knowing that they aren't the whole story is the key to moving beyond them. As a mother, she saw her children's potential, which enabled her to become the best advocate for them. She is proof that our greatest gifts might not all come wrapped in perfect packages, but when we embrace their unique talents and individuality, they have the potential to be the best gift we could ask for.*

## AN OPPORTUNITY IN DISGUISE

### James Blakemore

As an entrepreneur, I have a lot of experience. I became a part of the family oil and gas and ranching business right out of college. When I was 26, I bought my first business, a radio station. I started and ran my own commercial photography business. I ran a mining company for 20 years, taking it from worthless to a multi-million-dollar sale. In addition, I started an environmental remediation company, which was doing well until the supplier of our primary process ingredients folded, causing us to shut our business down.

For many years, I've been in the real estate development and rental property business and owning single and multi-family real estate properties. Every investment we made brought us a profit.

I was also part of a 100-year-old family business, which started with a sawmill that was acquired and owned by my great grandfather, who turned it into the largest lumber concern in the state of Texas. Along the way, he bought land, harvested the timber, and sold the surface and kept the minerals. From there, he got in the oil and gas, ranching, and capital businesses, which made him quite wealthy.

From that, I learned there is always an opportunity built into another opportunity. So no matter what business I was in, I was always looking to be an ethical opportunist. I guess I got that from my great granddad.

My great grandfather left his entire empire to his two sons, who continued their dad's success in the ranching and oil businesses, but not necessarily in the other businesses, divesting themselves of millions of dollars of other business interests because they couldn't agree on how to manage them.

When he died, my grandfather passed much of his businesses on to his two daughters and grandchildren; one of the daughters was my mom, and I was one of the grandchildren. We took our inheritance from his estate, and we also enjoyed success. At one point, we were one of the top five largest landowners in the state of Texas.

When my father passed, he left the family business to his five children. This afforded me the opportunity to have the revenue to live the life and lifestyle I've enjoyed for most of my life. Mostly, I enjoyed being an entrepreneur and have been successful in many ventures. Then something happened to change all that. The family-owned business that I depended on, but only owned a minority interest in, was being managed and operated in a way that was not to my advantage, actually to my detriment. Money that should have come to me was being diverted to other purposes. That mismanagement significantly impacted the cash flow coming in so negatively that the lifestyle I knew suddenly came to a screeching halt, almost to the point that I could see the skid marks on the asphalt. WTF?

I was blindsided, crushed, wondering how a family member, charged with operating the business for the benefit of all the siblings, could cause such irreparable damage to the family's legacy. I thought, what the fudge is going on here? Then when I figured out what had happened, I was left in shock, asking myself over and over, "What am I going to do? You could have rented me the decorations and party supplies, because I admit I had a pity party, albeit a fairly short one, while I pondered how this could have happened—how does a family member do this to another family member? The emotions were deep, and they burned. But I didn't let that go on too long, because in my life, I've always known there is a balancing and sometimes an even greater lesson or a gift within every challenge. This was no exception, and I knew I could overcome it—I just had to find the gift.

Standing in front of a mirror, metaphorically, I reflected on who I am and what I'd accomplished in 40-plus years. I had brought my entrepreneurial acumen to startups, joint ventures, coaching, and in supporting others, and I knew I had done them pretty good. Then I realized while I was doing that for everyone else, I wasn't doing it for me. I had applied everything I knew to helping others, but I wasn't using it to help myself, my wife, my family, and those closest to me.

I came to realize that I would not have realized this that had it not been for the WTF situation with the family business.

Like the cobbler whose children walk around with holes in their shoes, I needed to take care of me and mine.

Talking about shoes, I picked myself up by the bootstraps and took control of my life. I made a list of my skills, abilities, and successes. Then I made another list of the times when I'd fallen short. Happily, the first list was longer than the second.

Then I asked myself, what can I bring to my new endeavors to sustain and even multiply my lifestyle? I began that task with a big smile on my face, full of confidence and resonance, knowing full well that everything had led me to that day, including, and especially, the WTF moment that brought me to my OMG realization.

Today, I enjoy being an entrepreneur and operating my own businesses even more than before. I'm a success because all the knowledge and experience I've accumulated over the decades, the difference now is that I'm in control and my contribution and efforts benefit me, my family, those close to me, and even the world in general.

I'd always known what it took to be a successful entrepreneur, but this was the first time I was forced to apply what I knew to my own business and legacy.

Looking back, I realize that I almost lost the opportunity to benefit from my WTF, so what have I learned from it?

- Every disappointment carries within it the seeds of an equivalent or greater blessing and vice versa.
- The hand that inserts the knife in your back may belong

to someone that you love and trust and is smiling to your face the whole time.

- Never regret your past, as you are the sum of everything you have done or not done, and you will never know when these past experiences will be required to help move you along your journey.

- You are stronger, wiser, and more powerful than you ever give yourself credit for.

- It is never too late to start over, nor is it ever too late to create your masterpiece.

- Everyone is placed in your life for a reason, some good, some bad, but unfortunately people don't come with labels, so you may not know which they are until the lesson has been learned. BE CAREFUL!!

- …many, many more!

The LOL is how blessed I have been to have been adopted and selected into this family, a legacy family in the history of the Great State of Texas, that I've learned so much from my mother and father, who learned so much from their parents and grandparents, and that, in spite of all the machinations, manipulations and duplicity of an ethically challenged individual, I'm once again on top and looking to the stars for my next grand adventure.

I almost missed the opportunity to take everything I've learned from these people and apply it to create my own enterprise and masterpiece, and be able to provide for myself, my beloved wife, and family. I am so excited to be in the process of that right now as I renew my great grandfather's legacy within my own family.

# THE MORE YOU GIVE, THE MORE YOU GET

## David Stanley

Life was good. I was living in Carlsbad and had a beautiful girlfriend who I adored. I had a good team backing me and was working with studios on a project called Growing Up in Graceland. If there was anything wrong, it was that fact that I needed a knee replacement, and that was no surprise since I'd had problems since my days playing ball as a kid.

When I saw the doctor prior to my knee replacement, the doctor pointed out the fact that my hand was shaking. "You better get that checked out," he said.

In no hurry, I waited a month before I went to the doctor, who told me that I have Parkinson's disease, an incurable neurological disease. I said, "Let's get it fixed," to which he replied, "You can't get it fixed."

I had the knee replacement and found myself shaking more when I was in rehab. They gave me medication to help, but I was struggling. Not only couldn't I walk after surgery, but I now had an incurable disease, and that was affecting me psychologically.

As a man of faith, I was used to trusting in the Lord in all things, but I couldn't help but wonder what was going on. My faith was being tested, and I even thought I was going to shake, rattle, and roll, and then join my brother, Elvis.

My health declined. One day, I was drinking a glass of wine and took a couple pain pills to relax. Eight hours later, when I woke up, I was on the floor and the dog was licking my face. I had just had a stroke.

I know that God is in charge, and everything has a purpose. We may not like it, but He's up to something. I clung to my faith.

Well, things got worse with my Parkinson's, and psychologically, I got to the point where I wanted to give up. My relationship with my girlfriend fell apart, my health fell apart, and my film deals fell apart. The next thing I knew, I sold all my possessions and moved to Memphis to be with my brother.

I told God, "If you're trying to tell me something, tell me now."

Then something strange happened.

The first thing that happened that was encouraging was the birth of my granddaughter. It brought a glimmer of light, hope, and joy into my life. I knew then that I couldn't give up—I now had a reason.

Things were going well again, but then my brother, Ricky, suddenly died. He wasn't sick—I was the one who had an illness. Bewildered, I looked up to the heavens and asked my brothers, "Ricky, Elvis, what's up? What are you guys up to up there? What's this little game that we call life?"

Then, a friend invited me to stay with him in West Palm Beach, Florida, for a while. While I was there, I met Jim Gissy, who was second in command of the Westgate Resorts. Jim, who claimed to be the world's biggest Elvis Presley fan, wanted me to authenticate some of his Elvis memorabilia. He also wanted to introduce me to David Siegel, who owns the Westgate Resorts, particularly the one in Vegas that used to be the Hilton, where Elvis did so many shows, 827 shows to be exact. I was with him five out of the six years that he played there, and I knew the resort well.

I agreed to go to Vegas with him. When we pulled onto the tarmac, I had a flashback to the Elvis days when I caught a glimpse of the corporate jet that waited for us. When we walked through the hotel lobby, people started talking, openly pointing at me and saying that I was Elvis Presley's brother.

After it happened a few times, Jim pulled me aside. Standing in the lobby, next to the Elvis statue, he asked me if I wanted a job as the hotel's ambassador. OMG! Suddenly, I had a job, a suite at the Westgate, and I was meeting high rollers in the resort. I was finally getting stable and back on my feet!

But I still had Parkinson's disease.

One night, I was standing on my balcony, reflecting on what had brought me there. I suddenly realized, OMG, I had been in the wrong place at the wrong time. Now I was in the right place at the right time.

It filled me with gratitude.

As I looked out at the desert, I asked God what He was trying to say to me.

"I love you is what I'm trying to say," He replied. "I've given you the gift of communication and the platform to communicate your message all over the world, and that message is to love one another, forgive and forget, put others first, live in gratitude and love and care for people, just as I have done you."

I realized that He was right.

When I was brought to the desert, I had been a broken vessel. Today, my heart is full of joy and overflowing with gratitude. I am grateful to have the opportunity to share what God has put in my heart, and that's loving, caring, and prioritizing your life by making everyone else's life more important than your own. A sacrifice is giving more than you've got, but you've got so much more than you think you have. And the more you give, the more you get back.

I'm not done yet, and God isn't done with me. And I'll continue to be grateful for that every day.

*** 

*David says that God used Elvis's voice (specifically his gospel music) to deliver a powerful message, and He uses David's to communicate the same message—one of love, redemption, and gratitude. Today, David talks to people about his brother's soul, saying that Elvis was much more than a singer. He uses his gift from God to speak to the souls of the people he meets, reminding them they, too, are loved and have much to be grateful for.*

## A TEENAGE LOSS LEADS TO HEALTHFUL LONGEVITY

Phyllis Ayman

*1970*

A teenaged girl, age seventeen, was sitting on the front porch of her house on a warm spring evening the Monday before Father's Day. She was engrossed reading *The Godfather*. That teenage girl was me.

I can still see what I was wearing: the yellow blouse, green skirt, and colorful sash. My father was sitting next to me, and everything was calm and peaceful until I heard what sounded like a loud roar. Our next-door neighbor, my "Uncle" Sidney, jumped over the partition bricks that separated our two houses and started slapping my father in the face. He yelled at me to go inside and get my mother. I had no idea what was happening. I looked over and saw my father slumped over in the chair next to me. He appeared to be sleeping, and I thought maybe that "roar" was a "snore." But this was different. It was much louder, and there was only one, not like the incessant snoring I usually heard from my father when he was sleeping. I came to know it as what is called a "death rattle." In what seemed like forever but was really only a few minutes, there were sirens heading down the street. Firemen and policemen were standing on the porch over my father, who was now lying on the ground. They worked feverishly for almost an hour, but to me it seemed that in an instant, I was sitting next to a human being with no pulse. A human being that was no more . . . my father was gone.

I knew my father had a condition, but he was well cared for by doctors. He had been diagnosed with diabetes long before I was born. I grew up knowing there were special food restrictions and accommodations to be made for a person with diabetes. My mother cooked judiciously, sidestepping and substituting sugar in almost all dishes. When that wasn't possible, she always made something separately for my father.

As a matter of fact, I rarely remember any sugar in the house. I do remember vividly that there was always a bottle of Sucaryl, an artificial sweetener, on our dinner table and my father always used saccharin in his coffee. My mother wasn't a baker, so whenever we had store-bought cakes and pies, they were dietetic. Occasionally for a birthday or special celebration, my mother would buy two—one regular, the other dietetic.

But my father also didn't listen. He was a tyrannical, arrogant man. Knowing carbohydrates turn to sugar, he thought avoiding potatoes and rice were the only food items he had to eliminate. My mother would caution him against eating too much bread, pasta, and fatty foods such as cream cheese and sour cream, considered staples in the Jewish diet. He didn't listen. He would always argue. I can still hear the arguments now.

For most of my young years, he took Orinase, which belongs to a group of drugs called sulfonylureas that are used to treat type 2 diabetes. It helps to lower blood sugar by causing the pancreas to produce insulin (a natural substance that is needed to break down sugar in the body). It also helps the body use insulin efficiently. But in the year or two before this incident, he had to begin injecting himself with insulin.

Despite the diabetes, I never thought of my father as unwell. After all, he went to the doctor regularly for his checkups. The revered doctor, the man with the stethoscope and the white coat, a member of the U.S. medical community looked upon as having the most advanced medical care in the world, would surely protect my father.

We'd play catch, hit the penny, and stoop ball, favorite street games at the time. He taught me to ride a two-wheeled bicycle. We traveled by car from our modest Brooklyn home to New England and Canada and all the way to Florida. Whenever we were driving anywhere, I used to sit in the back seat behind my father and perch my head on the top of his seat, talking to him the whole way. He'd share the history of wherever we were going as well as his personal stories. I was truly "Daddy's Little Girl."

My father was an athlete when he was younger. My mother always told the story of his handball prowess from the time they were dating when he'd beat every other guy on the court. The story was always the same. Everyone else was running around like crazy, and my father seemed to be just standing there. My mother never understood it until one day someone who admired his skill explained that he was 'in control," a sort of master of the court, making everyone else run around.

I only understood this myself in later years. Handball, like most other games, is a game of angles. As an accountant, my father was aware of this. That's one of the reasons he excelled. He loved talking and thinking about numbers. As a matter of fact, all the men in his family in his generation and the one following were mathematicians and tax accountants. I'm pleased to say, however, that it stemmed from his mother, an immigrant to the U.S. from Russia. While she didn't speak English, read, or write, I was told that she ran a haberdashery store and was able to calculate sales and keep track of inventory, etc., all in her head.

My father had always expressed a burning desire to go to California and see the Pacific Ocean. We had taken many car trips, and my parents had traveled to Europe and Bermuda. But, oh, the West Coast, Big Sur, the Pacific Ocean—that was his dream.

He had a very mild heart attack six months prior to fulfilling this dream. I didn't find out until much later that my father was unwell several times on that trip. upon returning, he immediately went to the doctor, considered to be the savior.

When the doctor learned that my father took this trip without first consulting him, and hearing how unwell he was during the trip, the doctor apparently unceremoniously threw him out of his office and told him never to return. He told him that if he wasn't going to follow instructions, he could no longer be his patient. He essentially fired my father as his patient.

On that very warm spring night, seated next to me on the front porch, the system in which he and our entire family put our faith seemed to be failing him. It may have been considered the best in the world, but it didn't work in this case. What could have happened? He had just come home from the doctor, and then, in a matter of hours, he was gone.

I was sad, brokenhearted. I had just finished my first year of college. This was my father, the person I thought would proudly watch me graduate from college with honors, fulfill my professional career goals, walk me down the aisle and dance at my wedding the way we often practiced in our living room. He would delight in seeing his grandchildren and all of the life experiences that go along with that.

Beyond being sad and brokenhearted at a deep level, another component of my emotionality was my faith in the medical system. After all, we were so glad my father regularly went to the doctor. Did the system we put our faith in fail him?

Oddly enough, I pursued a career in the health sciences—in my particular case, speech and hearing.

After watching my mother care for my grandmother and helping to care for her for a two-week period when she was in a nursing home and my parents were on vacation, I found myself working as a speech/language pathologist in one of most egregious areas of the medical care system in America:

the nursing home industry.

My work has segued from caring for people in nursing homes to advocacy and nursing home reform, guiding people as a strategic advisor to make the best decisions for themselves or for their loved one's care, to the importance of self-care. I've realized that it wasn't the medical system that failed my father, but that on some level my father failed himself. He did not take full responsibility for his health condition. In not taking full responsibility, he also did not live up to the responsibility he had to his family—to care for himself in the best way he could.

I've worked over 40,000 hours with thousands of individuals and their families in over 50 of our nation's nursing homes in a career that spans forty-five years. I would have amassed a small fortune if I had even a dime for every person that told me they wished they had followed the doctor's instructions: took their blood pressure medication, followed their diabetic regimen, consistently followed through on prescribed treatments.

Of course, we all know of situations in which people are making what seem to be the best choices for their well-being, but through no fault of their own, environment, familial predisposition, etc., an illness befalls them. And in those cases, the medical science, the best and the brightest, can be there for them to the greatest degree possible. Is it always successful? Obviously not. Many people lose friends and families to disease processes that are beyond anyone's control.

Very recently someone contacted me after following my blog articles. He asked me, "How did you come to where you are in your thinking about mindful longevity and developing personalized longevity plan as part of aging life management?"

I gave him an answer, but it seemed there was something deeper; I just didn't know what it was. I thought, *how did I end up here?* When I started out in speech and hearing, I certainly never expected to wind up as the Ambassador of Conscious Aging Life Management.

I couldn't stop thinking about it. Did you ever have one of those nights when there are things on your mind that are still gnawing at you, and they wake you up in the middle of the night? But this question didn't wake me up in the middle of the night—this one kept me from falling asleep.

And then I experienced a eureka moment that shook me to my core, like a bolt of lightning coming through the window. I suddenly knew where it all started—it started with my father. *WTF, he failed himself! And in doing so, he failed us!*

I then realized, *OMG! I've been driven to make a difference, not only in a system that failed my father in some ways but also one that radically failed our family.* I don't know if that realization would have happened if, as a girl of 17, I hadn't in an instant come face-to-face with the trauma of my father's death.

My father was not uncommon. In our nation, we are expiring before our expiration dates are due. We spend money on prescription drugs, diets, fads. We're the most obese nation in the world. The American diet crisis consists of fats, fried food and oversized portions.

And now, working in the nursing home industry, I've not only been helping older adults, but also helping the seventeen-year-old daughter or granddaughter of the patient with whom I'm working.

At a deep level, I think it was the realization that when we put our faith in a system to care for us unequivocally, we look outside ourselves for the answers, the decisions, the treatments.

**Stay with me here . . . this is where the COVID-19 pandemic is an important part of the story. This is how and where IMpathy® was born and took on its wider meaning.**

I was retained as a consultant to conduct training on communication and empathy at a nursing home in upstate New York. During one of the sessions, as the attendees participated in an exercise, one of them said, "This is like empathy for yourself, inward empathy."

When I arrived home, I pondered and researched what he said. The only references for self-care, self-compassion, self-kindness, and self-forgiveness were self-empathy, which I thought was awkward. I created the word IMpathy®, and I now own the trademark for the word. It is what I call the inner game of empathy and the basis of a self-care commitment letter.

*March 2020*

During COVID I was covering as a speech/language pathologist in a small nursing home. While you've likely heard reports of how devastating it is to wear PPE for hours on end, unless you've experienced it, you can't even imagine. Sweating, shortness of breath, exhaustion! Many of my colleagues were at their wits' end. I reached out to several nursing home regional directors and COOs that I knew personally. I begged them to let me present a free thirty-minute webinar on techniques their staff could use to help reenergize and reinforce their strength. "You can't pour from an empty cup." I was repeatedly turned down. They just weren't interested. One actually told me, "I wouldn't want to watch a webinar because I have to wear a mask." I explained that he was in an administrative capacity, visiting a building for thirty minutes at a time, but that he had no idea what it was like for his staff who are working eight to sixteen-hour shifts wearing PPEs. It struck me that in actuality, within the nursing industry there seems to be a lack of empathy for the residents who are depending on them for care and empathy.

My work on IMpathy® was originally created for healthcare workers, then caregivers, but I've finally realized the importance this represents for us all.

**2022**

Words carry power. IMpathy ® and its meaning represents an important concept about self-care and responsibility. LOL, I don't know if I would have created it had I not had that experience with my father, along with a keen power of observation.

It's about assuming personal responsibility. We can't merely depend on doctors to prescribe medications that are supposed to help us feel better, cure our ailments, and eliminate our symptoms. In many ways they just mask the symptoms rather than cure the underlying condition. It is up to us to play an active role in that process.

Whatever you've become professionally or whatever role you play in your family and in your community, you are becoming what could affectionately be called an "Old Fart in Progress" (not to be confused with an ageist expression of an "old fart") — that is, if you play your cards right.

What has influenced my thinking is the important role of personal responsibility in healthful longevity so we can avoid becoming victims of the horrible nursing home industry that has not lived up to the promise of a dignified, respectful, purposeful life with quality care that we all deserve as we live to advanced years.

While most older adults don't think about or consider that they will be in a nursing home, the fact remains that approximately 40% of adult Medicare beneficiaries will spend at least some time in a nursing home and according to the U.S. Census Bureau, there are 10,000 people per day turning 65 between now and 2034.

One, therefore, could make the case that a commitment to health and well-being can be one of the greatest statements of personal responsibility one can make.

I challenge you to face your habits. Look them squarely in the face; honestly talk to them. Think about breaking habits that are not productive rather than becoming symptoms of them. Habits may likely be putting you very quickly in a place you would prefer not to be.

I look outward, but I also look inward. My father didn't look inward. He didn't consider that as the CEO of his own health and well-being, he would also be fulfilling a responsibility to his family. He was not only lying to us; he was lying to himself.

IMpathy® is about looking inside; about caring for ourselves. I have deep empathy for others, but also for myself. I'm not suggesting that we shouldn't care what others think or recommend, but most importantly it's what we think, and the choices we choose to make. That is the story of personal responsibility.

**The Wellness CEO – by Phyllis Ayman**

Your health is YOUR business.

Are you the keeper of your well-being?

It's NEVER too late.

The place to begin is within,

The time to begin is NOW!

Your Health is Your BUSINESS!

You are the CEO of your well-being.

If you don't mind, it doesn't matter, but

If you mind, make it MATTER!

IMpathy®

The Place to Begin is Within, The Time to Begin is NOW!!!!!

Recharge! Refresh! Reenergize!

Make the Rest of Your Life the Best of Your Life!

AGE MAGNIFICENTLY!

*** 

*Phyllis's experience shows just how our WTF moments can influence the trajectory of our lives. Her father's death was traumatic, and it had a profound and lifelong effect on her. It is undoubtedly impressive how the experience inspired her career choice and evolved into her quest to help others make life-changing health choices. While we cannot turn back time and change our WTF moments, Phyllis shows us that, oh my gosh, we can discover the hidden benefits in them.*

## A STROKE OF LUCK

### Mitch Axelrod

I woke up on March 27, and on that day, my life changed. Something was wrong, and I couldn't move my fingers. Immediately, the red flags went up and knew this could be serious. I called for help and said I thought I was having a stroke. When I fell, I *knew* I was having a stroke. When the emergency personnel arrived, I stumbled out to the ambulance, and I was suddenly paralyzed, unable to move at all.

"You're having a stroke," I was told. "Calm down, relax."

The rest of that day was a whirlwind, and I don't remember much of it. The next morning, the doctor talked to me and broke the news. He told me that the CT scan and MRI showed that I had a brain aneurysm, but surprisingly it wasn't related to my stroke. The aneurysm was on the right side, but the stroke came from my left side, which is why it paralyzed the right side of my body. The doctor said they had to operate on the aneurysm because if it should burst, I would be a dead man.

WTF? If a stroke wasn't enough, I now learn that I also had an aneurysm!

I had the first surgery the next day. I was awake for the surgery, and toward the end I heard the doctor say, "I got the sucker!" OMG, I thought, I'm going to live!

Well, the next day, the doctor informed me that they didn't get all of it, after all. They'd have to go back in again, this time with a laser directly into my head. Thankfully, this time, they were able to remove the entire aneurysm.

Nine weeks of in-house rehabilitation ensued. I had to relearn how to walk and talk. I also needed occupational therapy for my right arm. It was a tough time because I had to stay focus on me, but I was around so many people who were incapacitated and far worse than I was. I needed to keep my mental spirits up to stay focused on my health.

At the end of nine weeks, tests showed that I was well enough to go home. I had to prove that I could walk a mile with a 10-pound weight on my left hand to simulate shopping for groceries. I had to demonstrate that I could get in and out of the bathtub and be able to walk a 6-minute mile. When I passed, I was deemed capable of going home and taking care of myself.

That's when the real fun started. I had rehab two times a week for the next six months. Overall, I had about 200 therapy sessions, including speech, occupational, and physical therapy.

It wasn't until six months later that I actually began to move my arm.

Fast forward two years plus, and my speech is at 80 percent, and I can walk. I'll be strong enough to hold myself up and go skiing next year. There are areas where I still struggle. For example, I don't have fine motor skills, but I can move my fingers and pick up things. I can write, although I write very slowly, and I cannot yet type.

I may never regain all of my capabilities after the stroke, but I knew I couldn't be in recovery anymore. I got to the point where I said this is it—I'm back. Whatever faculties I have, I need to make the best of it.

As my son told me, "Dad, maybe this is the time for you to appreciate your body of work and not be obsessed about creating new work. Maybe get your existing work out."

That was a real turning point for me. It helped me shift my intention from constant creation to appreciation, looking back and seeing that I could appreciate the body of work that I had created. Maybe it was time to release that to the world.

That was a WTF! My son actually gave me my OMG!, showing me the lesson, the gift, that I had been waiting to receive.

I've had several WTFs that have turned into OMGs. Perhaps one of the greatest was that it was only because I had a stroke that I am alive today, for if I hadn't had that stroke, my brain aneurysm wouldn't have been found, and I would have died. I guess you could say that I had a stroke of luck. Who knows, maybe I could have lived to 100. Regardless, I was playing Russian roulette with a loaded chamber.

I am grateful to be alive and for the ability to do the things that I can do today. Little things like being able to pick something up have taken on a new meaning and importance in my life. My gratitude increases with each item on my checklist that I can now master and as I can recognize improvement in my abilities.

Having a stroke taught me how to stay present and curtail the little things that invite frustration every day. I no longer get upset when I knock something over. I appreciate what I do have, and I try not to take anything for granted.

People talk about being present, but it's very hard to be present. However, I've found that when I have to be present and focus on a task, it helps to stay present. You don't want to look too far ahead or risk thinking about what you might not be able to do in the future.

In the past, I didn't have that focus. Like many others, my mind used to project itself into the future. I did things that would get me to my goal. The stroke required me to focus on my role today. Role is always in the present, and a goal is always in the future. By shifting my intention to today's tasks, I very much grew to appreciate being in the present. Then with respect to my soul, I had to rely on the strength of my inner soul to build mental strength that I didn't know was in me. Today, I have more patience. I sit back and let things play out, rather than interceding and trying to force the outcome.

I'd always known about the importance of staying present. I've even talked about it. But never before had I experienced it at the level I am experiencing it today. I now know that I hadn't understood the concept at this level before. Whether I had a stroke so I could learn that, I don't know. But the fact that I have learned it has fortified me every day since then, and I am more consciously aware of the importance to integrate it into my everyday life.

Well, I don't know that there's anything funny about having a stroke, but perhaps my LOL is in the beauty of knowing I can laugh out loud. Oh, my smile isn't as broad as it used to be, but I am laughing out loud, perhaps louder than ever before. And it's all because I have a newfound perspective and appreciation for life and the things that are so easily taken for granted.

Yes, LOL, I have a stroke to thank for that.

## HAPPY RE-BIRTHDAY TO ME

### Alec Stern

Today, October 23, 2020, is my two-year Re-Birthday. It was on this day, in 2018, I checked into the hospital for a "routine robotic surgery," and, let's just say, I died and came back…

This story begins in early 2018. I had an amazing nurse practitioner who had switched practices around 2013. The location of her new practice was too far away for me so, for about five years, I saw a doctor closer to me. Over this time, my new doctor opted not to run a PSA test, and I honestly didn't know enough at the time to ask that this be done. The PSA test is a blood test used primarily to screen for prostate cancer. The test measures the amount of prostate-specific antigen (PSA) in your blood.

When my nurse practitioner moved again to a practice close to me, I switched to this practice. She initially did a full work up and assessment on me, which included a PSA test. The results came back, and my PSA level was 4.2. After culturing, it was 4.9. (A 0 score is no presence of cancer). Now, 4.9 seemed like a low number to me but, without any PSA test history to compare this to, my nurse practitioner referred me to a specialist to biopsy my prostate just to be safe. I headed to the doctor to get my biopsy results. When I sat down, the doctor said, "How are you? You have cancer." I actually laughed and said, "Wow, that was so quick and to the point. That's like saying, how's your day? You have cancer. How about them Red Sox? You have cancer." We laughed about this, but I really appreciated the direct approach with no long buildup to my results.

**How Serious is It?**

While prostate cancer *is* a more manageable cancer that grows slowly, I had 7 out of 12 biopsies with cancer, with a few being 90% cancer and near the edge of the prostate, which means cancer cells could be present outside of the prostate. If so, it potentially, would not be so manageable. Ultimately, I was diagnosed with Stage 3, Advanced Prostate Cancer. While this news isn't the kind anyone wants to hear, my first reaction was, "I got this!" I was determined not to let cancer hold me back! Like others, I have had many life obstacles I have had to overcome, and this was the next one I needed to beat.

My goal was to see the top doctors in urology, oncology, and radiology. Of course, none of them were accepting new patients. But I reached out to them and my network and became their new patient. I won't go into too much detail but after a lot of research, talking to doctors, and people in my inner circle, there were six options for me initially, which narrowed to the two options I could consider for my unique situation. I decided my best course of action was robotic surgery.

The surgery was set for October 23, 2018. I didn't want to burden anyone and thought I'd just head to the hospital by myself, stay a few days and Uber home. If I needed help, I would seek options then. But a dear friend insisted on coming up from New Jersey to stay with me for a few weeks during my initial recovery. He put his busy life on hold to help me out. My sister also wanted to be there when I woke from surgery to make sure all was good. I was, and remain, touched by their willingness to be there for me.

**"Routine" Surgery – Ha!**

Early morning on October 23, 2018, I was off to the hospital for a "routine five-hour robotic surgery." When I signed the release, I even joked about the line: "this procedure could result in death." I would not think this was funny later.

As I was being prepped and given anesthesia, I joked with the doctors about wanting to see the maintenance records of the robot. I went under anesthesia, smiling, laughing and high fiving the doctor. I was ready to own this surgery. As I often say, "It was go time!"

Twenty-five hours later, I awoke from my five-hour surgery, which actually took nine hours due to major complications. I remember looking around and thinking to myself, "This looks anything but routine. There were 10 people in my room, IVs of blood and machines beeping all around me… My lead doctor, the Chief of Urology, informed me that I had died on the operating table and they brought me back. Imagine that! I couldn't grasp this at all. I thought, "How is this possible with a routine surgery and literally millions of these procedures performed each year?" As it was explained to me, a blood vessel burst and, because it was tucked up under my pelvic bone, they couldn't reach it to stop the bleeding. As I literally bled to death, I went into cardiac arrest, needing to be fully resuscitated while they replaced 120% of my blood to save my life.

My expected two days in the hospital and two weeks at home turned into my being in the ICU for two days, being ambulanced to another part of the hospital, a nine-day hospital stay, and a ten-week recovery. This was one of the hardest things I've ever been through in my life—and it could've broken me. I had a choice to make, and I decided to kick all this to the curb! I was given a new lease on life.

**Lessons to Share**

As reflect on my two-year Re-Birthday, I wanted to share a few lessons I learned (and earned):

- Telling friends and family you have cancer is not an easy thing to do (or hear). Personally, I wanted my friends to just listen, empathize, and support me. When someone informs you they have cancer, you don't have to say you are sorry; you don't have to tell stories about people in your life who have battled cancer. Just listen, empathize, and show your love and support. Some of the things people said to me were not comforting or helpful as they were intended to be. "My dad had that cancer, and it was no big deal." Or "My aunt had cancer, and she died." If you feel compelled to share a story, it's better to hear a survivor story vs. a minimalization or a terrible ending.

- Everyone's experience is different. All cancers are different. I know there are many people that are battling ones bigger than mine, but please don't say, "If you are going to get cancer, this is a good one to get."

- You may not want to ask people for help. You may intend only to inform them of your situation. My advice is to accept their desire and willingness to be there for you, care for you, and help you in any way.

- You may discover that having cancer is a great check in that reveals who in your life is important, which friends should remain in your life and which ones it's time to cut loose. I sadly severed ties with some of my past close friends because, while I wasn't asking for anything, they could not be present. They could not make the time to hear what I was going through, and one or two of them summarily discounted what I was dealing with.

- On the flip side, there were some newer friends in my life that surprised me by going above and beyond. I remain touched by their presence and the many ways in which they stepped up and supported me. Several of these friends are now my besties.

- I believe someone (she) up there decided it wasn't time for me to go. I feel I was brought back to continue my journey and to empower others, and I don't take one minute for granted.

- I am often asked if I saw a bright light when I stopped breathing in the midst of surgery. When I went under anesthesia, I was happy, joking, ready and confident. I was completely unconscious when I went into cardiac arrest, so I didn't see lights or hear angels singing (or devils cheering).

- This is a PSA Announcement for PSA tests. Guys get your PSA tests done and don't put them off. While there are different schools of thought about PSA testing, I'm glad I did it because an early diagnosis can be managed.

- While it was indescribably tough to go through a 10-week recovery, I had to make a choice: Let it bring me down, own me, and define me or stay strong and fight. I chose the latter and treated cancer like I do with other challenges in life; it was just another obstacle that I needed to tackle and kick to the curb.

- Find a way to incorporate humor and laughter on this journey. I was determined not to let cancer define me or change the relationships I have with others. With the stress and unknowns of cancer you will naturally experience many highs and lows. Humor and laughter can lift you up, as well as others around you. I wanted to be sure I didn't allow cancer to change my approach to life or change my relationships and interactions with others. My friends and family could always rely on my quick wit and dry sense of humor and, if I wasn't being me, that only saddened me and others.

Today, two years later, there's a 70% probability I am cancer free! Since my cancer had poked out of the prostate and cancer cells could be present, I now get a PSA test every six months and will do so for the rest of my life. I set my intentions and visualize my PSA test results are zero and will remain zero forever!

I waited until I was really ready to tell my story. It's my hope that, by sharing it now, I can help others. In fact, I am a contributing author to the best-selling book, ***1 Habit to Beat Cancer: Secrets of the Happiest Cancer Thrivers on the Planet,*** which is an inspirational book to read. Check it out on Amazon: https://www.amazon.com/Habit-Beat-Cancer-Happiest-Thrivers/dp/B08749ZSL9

# A FIVE-DIAMOND TRANSFORMATION

## Carlos Bueno

The Newbury Hotel first opened in 1927 as one of the first Ritz Carlton hotels in the country. In the ten years ending in 2019, our hotel was at the bottom of the luxury set in the city of Boston. It was a beloved hotel and icon that had fallen on some very difficult times for a multitude of reasons. At that time, it was at the end of its lifetime.

We were incredibly fortunate that our ownership group recognized the potential of the property and, more important, the potential of the associates in the building. However, the product did not match the service. Our principals also acknowledged that the asset itself contained beauty and infinity within the city of Boston that gave us a fantastic opportunity to introduce and launch a new brand.

The property closed in 2019 with the intention of opening in spring 2020. When we closed, there were approximately 150 associates and managers in various departments that believed enough in the brand that we were launching that they decided to stay with the project, despite the time off.

One of the most remarkable aspects of our ownership team is that when the property closed in 2019, the group worked with the associates to create a safety net that would at least support the associates through the renovation period. One of the key components was providing health insurance coverage for all of our associates while they were away from work.

Late in 2019 and early in 2020, there were some delays in construction that delayed our opening. We were likely now looking at opening in mid-summer or toward the end of that year. This created some distrust because our employees and associates were looking forward to returning in March.

From that point, we experienced a domino effect of WTF. I was thinking WTF is going on with all these delays? We've made a commitment to the market and the associates, and now we had to tell them, no, we won't be opening on time. Then the associates were thinking, what the fudge? I might have been able to do something else, but I believed in you and the brand, and now we are delayed!

We had been certain we would open in March, and now just 90 days into the project, it would be June, potentially September. It appeared that we might have done a bait and switch, and for that, I felt responsible. I had 150 families that were counting on us to pay their bills and their mortgage. I also knew that they had other opportunities, but because they believed in us, they turned them down.

I knew it was out of our control, but even if our associates knew that, too, it didn't make it any better.

Unfortunately, as March rolled around and we began to hear news of a fire that was spreading around the world and making its way to the city of Boston, that concern quickly shifted. No longer was there concern about if and when the hotel would open—the concern shifted toward the health of our associates and their families, and COVID impacted our community and the world.

The other thing that changed is that we were having meetings and communications differently. No longer able to meet face to face, our meetings were replaced with audio and visual conversations. We began to see each other in our homes, wearing casual clothing and seeing how our families were doing.

By the time June and July came around, we had the commitment that the project would be finished and we could open the project together at some point. We made a commitment to take every precaution possible to make sure the building would be safe, whatever that would be deemed to be, when it was open to the public and our employees.

Initially, we expected to be closed for five months. Ultimately, we were closed for nineteen months, and during the entire time, the ownership was true to its promise to provide both the employer and employee contribution toward health insurance. When the commitment was made, we didn't know that a pandemic was around the corner, and we certainly didn't envision the massive extension of time that we would be obligated to continue with that coverage. These were just a few of the WTFs that were experienced during the renovation.

When the transition team came in, our Zoom and Go-to meetings became much more personalized. We wanted to understand how safe each other's families were and if there was any additional outreach we could do. Things began to improve as vaccines rolled out. In late 2020 and early 2021, we also began to train via Zoom.

In hospitality, so much is about connection and being in front of each other. Of the 150 associates, a good portion of them who had tenure anywhere from 5 years to 34 years of service in the building, were able to guide us in a Zoom setting through each of the rooms. Our front office team knew each of the rooms, and they became mentors for the new associates we brought on board.

Our associates were the most committed and loyal. The entire population allowed us to reposition ourselves as the premier luxury hotel in Boston and be recognized not only in our community, but globally. In less than one year of operation, we received AAA five diamond designation and have been named the top hotel in the city by a number of publications.

Oh, there were so many setbacks, so much strife, and so much heartbreak. Our owners went through so much money, and we all had our share of worries. The WTFs were plenty. But when we opened as perhaps the most united team of associates, from managers and leaders to everyone in between, we thought to ourselves, OMG! We could never have opened at this level if we hadn't gone through everything we went through.

Then fate gave us another OMG when we opened on the very

same date that the hotel had first opened its doors in 1927. This time, we opened with accolades that fill us all with a sense of pride.

That is who we are at the Newbury. The ownership, leadership, and every person who has been part of our renovation has displayed a level of commitment that goes beyond expectations. From our front desk to the board room and at every touch point in between, we have been blessed.

I offer my gratitude to each and every one of the associates with whom I've had the honor of working, both then and now, to build the Newbury to OMG, especially when we were dealt with so many WTFs.

The inspiration, confidence, and energy were definitely driven by our associates. However, I would be remiss if I didn't state that I was empowered by Mahmood Khimji, Principal at Highgate, who, throughout the pandemic, remained committed and connected with us. Anytime we had doubts, he was in our corner, even from afar. There was always the sense that, with his word, what I was representing to our associates was true.

***

*The Newbury Hotel in Boston is breathtakingly magnificent. Its history and architecture have been preserved and enhanced by its newfound elegance. Despite the many WTF setbacks, Carlos and his stellar team managed to create an experience that will make every guest stand in awe and say, OMG! from the moment they walk into the door.*

# LEANING IN

## Peter Katz

Most of my career has been spent as a touring singer-songwriter, travelling in a van across North America and Europe—sometimes beyond—and sharing my songs and stories. And while storytelling was always a big part of what I did on stage, the idea of being a keynote speaker to companies and organizations wasn't anywhere on my radar.

That is, until December of 2016.

A friend of mine was hosting an annual gratitude and appreciation event, and I was the first person to buy a ticket. He immediately messaged me with a proposal: I could attend the event for free if I'd agree to appear on stage at the end of the night, "say something" and play one of my songs to wrap things up. Of course, I said yes. Free ticket—and I love being given the opportunity to play!

At the end of that performance, a woman from the audience approached me. "Hey, that was amazing," she said. "I'm involved with a pretty special conference for tech startups and entrepreneurs. You need to come and give a keynote!"

She pitched me to the person who ran the conference—let's call him Sam—and I learned that one of his favorite songs of all time was one I had written ("The Camp Song"). All sorts of experienced speakers and company leaders were slated to speak at the conference, but Sam gave me the prime spot. Saturday night, 8 pm, I was going to be the event's closing speaker.

I recognized that this opportunity had the potential to be life changing, but I also knew that I had never given a keynote speech to "grown-ups" before, and especially not to an audience of 500 serious movers and shakers in the tech and business world. I had given a few keynotes to high school audiences, but the pressure of this event was on an entirely different scale.

With several months of lead time, I dove into preparing and researching how to create a transformative speech for the attendees of the conference. I recognized early on that these were "my people." Sure, they were entrepreneurs and I was a touring singer-songwriter, but there is a significant overlap between the life of an entrepreneur and the life of an artist.

Neither of us has a steady paycheck or set hours, and we're both deeply passionate about this "thing" we're trying to create out of nothing, all while needing to accept the intense risks and sacrifices required to find success—if we find it at all.

My golden rule around taking on big opportunities is to be incredibly prepared so I can be totally present in the moment. I know from my years of experience on stage that, more than anything that I'm saying, singing, or playing, being present and in the moment with my audience is the best way to make sure an event feels special and creates a significant impact. So, I got to work: I booked meetings with everyone I knew who was a professional speaker to pick their brains and soak up their wisdom; I took entrepreneur friends out for dinners to hear what their lives were like. I listened. I took notes. Slowly, but surely, I built my presentation over the course of several months.

In the fall of 2017, I arrived at the start of the four-day conference, three days before the big talk. Over the course of the next three days, I was deeply focused on the mission at hand, determined to get a clear sense of the people who would be in my audience. I had intentional conversations with anyone I crossed paths with, trying to gauge the mood of the room and to gather insights and stories on what mattered most to each attendee. Every night, I ducked out early, went back to my room, and worked and re-worked my presentation.

It's important to note that I have a degree in theater performance, so I always think about the overall experience of a presentation, not just the content. When I prepare for an event, I'm not only focused on what I'm saying or what song I'm playing; I'm thinking deeply about what the audience will feel. Sam had told me that he wanted the conference to feel "stripped down," purposely devoid of props and elaborate backgrounds—which I fully supported. But in my mind, there was a "sweet spot" to be found as far as curating a physical space that would be conducive to the kind of experience I wanted to create. I had already gently pushed back and requested to do my speech in a space with walls, rather than outdoors before a roaring campfire. I knew that my talk would require a certain focus and intimacy, and so Sam agreed to schedule me into one of his indoor spaces

When I arrived, the venue was empty: four walls, a wooden floor—barebones. In alignment with Sam's vision for the event, there were no stage lights or microphones in the space. However, my instincts were telling me that I needed amplification and that the right lighting would lend a "magic" of sorts to the space itself. Though I hadn't done a keynote like that before, I *had* done thousands of concerts in every venue imaginable, and I knew what would be necessary.

So, I got to work, keeping my mission in mind. I found some venue staff and inquired about lights, asked if I could borrow a microphone and some speakers, and, slowly but surely, I gathered all the equipment I needed. I even went around the whole venue, finding floor mats and cushions, anything I could do to create just the right vibe. When I had everything in hand, I set up the space, complete with additional lights I had brought from home. Hours later, I placed the final cushion, looked around … and everything was perfect. I was ready to go.

When Sam walked in two hours before my talk was scheduled to begin and saw what I had done, he freaked out. In his mind, I had violated the spirit of the conference. It was not the vision he had created, and he was upset.

He told me to tear it down.

WTF is going on here, I thought … and what am I going to do? I had worked for months preparing for this moment. I was confident my presentation could be transformative for the audience and that it would likely change both my life and Sam's if I could pull it off.

And now I was being told to take it all down?!

I'm generally a highly agreeable and accommodating guy. When confronted with something like this in the past, I likely would have backed down, compromised on my vision, and settled into the habit and comfort of people pleasing. Standing in front of Sam, I could feel that instinct bubbling up inside. I understood that he had a vision, too. Who was I to go against that? But it felt undeniably clear that an exception had to be made for my session. (Plus, I felt that my plan *was* actually aligned with his vision; he just didn't realize it yet.) When I'm sure of something, I'm sure of it. I knew, deep in my gut, my approach was the way it needed to be for the audience to have the experience I had worked so hard to create for them.

Sam was clearly in a state of overwhelm, and I had to carefully navigate this moment in order to keep things as I'd arranged them.

I suggested that we take a five-minute break so that he could catch his breath. When I approached him again, I very calmly but assertively said, "Do you trust me?"

He nodded.

"Okay, then. Whatever expectations you have about my session," I said, "I'm going to blow them right out of the water. However, I need you to let me do my thing." And like Obi-Wan Kenobi saying, "These aren't the droids you're looking for" in

*Star Wars*, I looked him right in the eyes, and with the calmest confidence I could muster, I said, "I'm going to do this my way, and I can't wait to see how happy you're going to be afterwards."

To Sam's great credit, he nodded again, put the event in my hands, and stepped back.

As the audience began to trickle in, there was a new sanctity within the space. Even before I'd said or done anything at all, I could sense a beautiful shift in our collective energy, and I knew that the audience could feel it, too.

Over the course of the next hour, I gave my first proper "keynote concert" (for "grown-ups"), and as I did, I felt 500 people lean in. They were with me for every word. When I was done, there was a bursting standing ovation.

After all the hugs and beautiful conversations with people afterwards, Sam walked up to me, tears streaming down his face. "Thank you," he said, hugging me. "Thank you, thank you, thank you."

A week later, as a result of the buzz generated by the event, I was called to meet with one of the biggest speaking agencies in Canada. They're now my agents, and with their support, I regularly deliver "keynote concerts" to businesses, organizations, and governments around the world. None of this would have happened if I hadn't stayed true to my vision and held my ground, gently but assertively ensuring that things happened the way I knew they needed to happen.

One of the great revelations of this experience came from that moment when I felt everyone *lean in*. That was when I realized that everything I had done up to that point in my life had left me perfectly qualified to do this thing—keynote speaking for companies and organizations—that I'd never imagined I could do.

I had previously thought that the only way for me to connect with people's hearts and minds was through something called "a concert." I had no idea I could connect with people as a speaker, too. This pivotal discovery allowed me to begin a new chapter of my career and develop a powerful, dynamic, and wholehearted way to interact with an audience.

My "OMG moment" came when I trusted my instincts, confident in myself and my vision. Standing in my truth allowed me to best serve Sam, his clients, myself, and all those who would later hear about what we had created together at my inaugural keynote. It was a departure from how I would have responded in the past, which would have been to compromise my integrity and politely agree to a lesser version of my plan.

The result was so monumental that it changed my life. Had I sold myself short and not stepped into my power, I would have missed the opportunity that has since allowed me to connect with and speak to more than 200,000 people over the last few years.

Once you have found your truth, stand strong in it. And when confronted with a "WTF" situation, go deep, lean in, and trust that there is an "OMG" lesson buried within that moment, waiting to be discovered.

## SURVIVING 9/11

### Greg Zlevor

The Singapore government and the Singapore Police Force are my clients. I had a flight scheduled for a trip to Singapore on the morning of Tuesday, September 11, 2001.

Two weeks prior to that trip, I found out from Susan, who was going to be my consulting partner on the project, that she was going to have an operation on the day we returned from Singapore. I told her that she couldn't do that—she was either going to have to reschedule the operation or she wouldn't be able to go on this trip. She wanted to go on the trip, but I refused and took her off the trip.

In her place, I brought a gentleman named Chris. I called the travel agent and told her that I knew she had me flying on United leaving out of Boston. "Is it possible that you can connect me with Chris, who is flying out of San Francisco so we can travel and fly together?" I asked.

He replied that he could put me on the American flight out of Boston or the 9:30 flight out of Chicago. I told him to look at the flights and make the decision. A couple days later, he called me back and told me he had put me on the flight out of Chicago.

Driving into Logan on the morning of 9/11, I heard that a plane has hit the tower. OMG! By the time I actually got to the airport, a second plane had hit the tower, and a plane had crashed in Pennsylvania.

By now, everyone is talking on the phone and wondering what was happening. There was talk that our nation was under attack, and all of the agents disappeared from the gates. When they finally reemerged, they announced that the airport was closed and told us that we all needed to go home.

The people in line started helping each other out, offering to get them a hotel or let them stay at their homes. I offered our house to a couple people, though no one took me up on it.

When I got home that afternoon, I turned on the TV, like most people did that day. When they put up a square listing the four flights that had been in the attacks that day, I realized that I had a ticket on the United flight. When I saw the American flight, I knew that I had almost been put on that flight. I think I might have been the only planet who had a ticket on both flights. I can't imagine that there was anyone else who could have said that.

I didn't talk for three days. And during those three days, I forgot to call Singapore to tell them I wasn't going to be there. When I finally did make that call, they told me they thought I had been on the plane and were, therefore, afraid to call me. I apologized and told them I was safe, but I didn't have much else to say.

During those three days, it occurred to me that my wife never told me she was glad I wasn't on that plane. Unfortunately, while I was so thankful I wasn't on either of those planes, I realized that I didn't have intimacy in my life. And I knew that I didn't want to spend the rest of my life without it. It was a very powerful and pivotal moment.

OMG, it was only because of chance that I didn't perish on 9/11, and it took this experience to bring to my attention the fact that we didn't have the intimacy and relationship that were important to me and my soul.

It wasn't until five years later that my wife and I finally separated. We went through five years of challenges and pain before I finally took action to end the marriage. Because I have a lot of compassion for people, decisions of this magnitude aren't always so easy to make. I love my kids and doing things with them. I loved coaching their teams when I could and taking them on trips. At that time, I couldn't see myself breaking up my family.

In that moment, not only was there not enough intimacy, there was virtually no intimacy at all. In my estimation, I was fighting for my soul every week, just trying to protect it, nurture it, and take care of it. I didn't have an ally; I had someone I felt I needed to protect myself from.

It just clicked that I couldn't go through life like that.

Later, I admitted to my wife that I was in pain. We went through six counselors, and that didn't help. I sought intimacy outside of the relationship, and I didn't like that, either. I didn't want to do that anymore and begged for her to help me fix our relationship.

It was a long, painful process, but I had to go through this experience in order to get out a dysfunctional marriage. I had to come face to face with the fact that I somehow managed to escape death on the morning of 9/11 to realize that my marriage was one in name only. Then I had to work through emotions and the turmoil and, yes, the mess in order to free myself of my pain so I could be able to have the type of relationship that I wanted — one that nurtured me and wouldn't hurt me.

My WTF moment was a significant and unforgettable moment in my life, as I'm sure it was for millions of others. But without it, perhaps I wouldn't have come to the realization that I wanted more in a relationship, in my marriage, and in life than what I was receiving. Coming to that realization has been the hidden blessing in the midst of an incredible tragedy.

For some reason, my life was spared that day, and I don't want to waste a moment of it. We never know what is going to happen, which is why I want to embrace the life I want today.

## ON THE FLIP SIDE OF FAME

### Chris Naugle

When I left Wall Street in 2018, my wife and I had been working for several years to get a show on HGTV and had just gotten our big break.

We were the number two show coming out. We were the reigning champs. Lowes wanted to be our sponsor, and we had endorsement offers.

We aired six times, and we got great ratings. We were getting all the rah rahs and pats on the butt. And then in our final airing, the ratings came out and were good, not great, but good enough. The producers told us it was fine, that maybe it was just a nice day and there weren't as many people watching.

I'll never forget the night. I was driving home in my black GMC when my phone rang. I looked down to see it was my producer. I felt overwhelming joy because I had been waiting for this call, the are you guys ready? Let's do this! That call.

But I immediately noticed that his tone was different. And all of a sudden, he told me that they decided not to move forward with our show.

Everything in my life had built up to this one climax moment. At that point, it was the only thing we'd been working toward. We had put our heart and soul into it, and I had left Wall Street for this moment. I had put everything into the line for this moment, and boom, it was over.

Discovery bought HGTV and froze all new shows. We just so happened to make it through this whole thing before they displaced everyone who was there and decided they were going to go deeper with existing shows. Then all that time, energy, effort, and dreams were shattered.

The first thing that came to my mind was whether I should just hit the gas and drive my truck into the tree to my right. I didn't know how I was going to go home and break the news to my wife, who had been dreaming of this moment by my side since 2014. I didn't know what to do.

When I got home, I told my wife the news, and she handled it better than I expected, though I could see the tears begin to well in her eyes.

Then my phone rang again. Not in the mood to take the call, I saw that it was from Greg, someone I had been working with and who was going to be one of the sponsors for the show. He'd been one of our biggest cheerleaders and best friends through the whole process.

When I answered, he was so positive and happy, saying that he was so excited that we were going to work together and how amazing it was going to be.

"Greg, we didn't get the show," I said. I didn't get the big break. I didn't get the show. I had nothing to offer anyone in the world because our show just got canned.

He said, "Chris, I'm calling because I'm excited about the things we're doing. The thing you have to understand in life is that sometimes one door closes so another door can open. The door is open—you just have to walk through it."

The door he referred to are the things that we are doing today, and Greg is my company partner who is helping do them.

That was one of the darkest times in my life. I didn't have an exit strategy. I had left my job at Wall Street that paid me high six figures. I had asked the compliance officer for an OBA, an outside business activity, so I could have an HGTV flipping show, and her answer was no. I had to make a decision to be a financial adviser or a TV show star. Right there, the decision seemed to be an easy one. I left everything I had known for 16 years.

When the unthinkable happened, I had my WTF moment.

Everything I'm doing today, travelling, speaking, and helping tens of thousands of people solve their money problems, none of that would have happened if we had that TV show. What we have now has far more longevity and helps far more people than a TV show could.

OMG, I now realize that when that door closed, it was the greatest gift God could have given me because it opened the door for what I am doing today.

The first time I realized that losing the show was a gift was when we went out to dinner with Brent, my current mentor and partner. At this dinner, he looked exhausted. My wife had been telling me that I needed to help him, but I had different agendas. When I didn't say anything, my wife quite obviously kicked me under the table. When Brent noticed, my wife spoke up, saying that I wanted to know if he needed help.

When I flew out to help him help him build the business, we laid out everything we do today, and it became crystal clear that this was what I was supposed to do.

This affirmation was reinforced when my wife and I recently did a flip, which we rarely do anymore. It was a beautiful house, and we put it on the market at a low price. After 120 showings, we got three offers, and none of them were any good. In the end, we did get a full price offer, which meant that we would get next to nothing. It was just one more sign that we weren't meant to be in real estate. It's not my calling, but what I do today is.

The easiest summary of this might be that in life we have to come to the conclusion that we need to solve other people's problems before we can solve ours. Up to that point, everything I had done was to solve my problems and feed my ego. Someone else was always second. At the point when I was staring down the opportunity with Brent, I had to help him. I had to give first in order to get, which might have been my biggest OMG takeaway.

I had my five minutes of fame, but now I have created a lifetime of success by helping people. And I wouldn't flip that for anything in the world.

# IT'S NEVER TOO LATE

## David Corbin

I was a 35-year-old husband and the father of a beautiful, bright 5-year-old daughter. The publishing-based media company that I created with $100 was four years old and, through the efforts of our 40 awesome salespeople, had expanded into its 14th state, doubling every year.

That's when our bank called in a substantial loan, and we were financially paralyzed. We couldn't function without our line of credit. We hadn't created a strategic plan or done a SWOT analysis. We kept saying that we didn't have the time to do those things because we were focused on making sales.

The truth is, we knew very little about running a business. We were great at sales and motivating salespeople, but we had not taken inventory of what we really needed to know to run a business of this magnitude.

So now that the bank was closing our line of credit, we were done. We were either going broke or forced to sell the business. It was beyond scary; it was debilitating. Yet there was no time to waste, we needed to find a buyer or face massive pain, bankruptcy, shame, and loss.

I couldn't share my angst with my wife because she was pregnant and had two previous miscarriages. I couldn't tell her it looked like we were going to lose our home to the bank. Every time I thought of my predicament, I quickly became nauseous.

Somehow, in the end, we were able to sell the business to a multi-national, billion-dollar company, and as part of the transaction, I had to stay on as President for a year. It sucked even after I sold the business.

OMG: After working with that new company, I came to see that there were so many areas of business that I was either completely ignorant about or less skilled than necessary to fulfill the needs of my entrepreneurial ventures.

Had I been more skilled in these areas, I would have been able to sell my business for millions—and it was clear to me that my 'ignorance' cost me literally millions of dollars! What a gift it was for me to be in that situation, to build a business beyond our ability to manage and grow, suddenly need to sell it, and then sell it to a European-based company that ran their businesses by the book. It put me in a position to learn what I needed to know, to gain insight into what I didn't know, and to understand the importance of closing those gaps. WHAT A BLESSING.

Had it not been for my stunning and jarring WTF situation, I might never have experienced my OMG epiphany.

Frankly, it wasn't until I was teaching what I had learned that I came to this realization and, with deep gratitude and appreciation for the experience, that I laughed and celebrated my WTF to OMG.

All's well that ends well, and a lesson learned in need is a valued lesson, indeed.

## ABOUT DAVID CORBIN

David Corbin has been referred to as "Robin Williams with an MBA" because of his very practical, high-content speeches, coupled with entertaining and sometimes side-splitting stories and applications. A former psychotherapist, he has served as a management and leadership consultant to businesses and organizations of all sizes—from Fortune 20 companies to businesses with less than one million—and enjoys the challenges of all. He has worked directly with the offices of the presidents of companies such as AT&T, Hallmark, Sprint, as well as the Hon. Secretary of Veterans Administration and others.

Davidcorbin.com

david@davidcorbin.com

## ABOUT KERRY JACOBSON

Kerry Jacobson has spent 20+ years as a Marketing and Sales expert in publishing-related fields. Early in his career, Mr. Jacobson ran sales divisions for magazines, including *Fortune, MIT's Technology Review, Information Week, Oracle Magazine, American Way* and *United in-flight* magazines, to name a few. He has taught specialized marketing classes at Harvard, MIT, UMass and U.R.I.

In 1995, Mr. Jacobson focused on book publishing, primarily on the "ebook" category. Over the past 15 years, he has had more WSJ, NYT & USA Today bestselling authors than any marketer on the planet! Primarily focused on business, self-help, and health books, Kerry selectively represents both traditional and independently published authors.

# OUR FEATURED AUTHORS

## (in order of appearance)

**Neary Heng (page 7):**

Neary Heng immigrated to the US in 1987 from war-torn Cambodia. After learning English, she became the first in her lineage to earn a college degree. Neary later applied her hard-earned lessons to become a high achiever in corporate America. She left the corporate world and started her own business to improve speeches and training around her proven strategies on purpose, harmony, and productivity. Visit NearyHeng.com

**Scott Parazynski (page 14)**

Dr. Scott Parazynski is a highly decorated physician, astronaut, best-selling author "The Sky Below," and tech CEO. He is a keynote speaker on innovation, risk management, mentorship, and leadership under extreme adversity. A graduate of Stanford University and Medical

School, he trained at Harvard and in Denver for a career in emergency medicine and trauma. In 1992, he was selected to join NASA's Astronaut Corps and eventually flew 5 Space Shuttle missions and conducted 7 spacewalks. In October 2007, Scott led the spacewalking team on STS-120, during which he performed 4 EVAs. He was inducted into the US Astronaut Hall of Fame in 2016. In addition to being a diver and accomplished mountaineer, he is also a commercial, instrument, multiengine and seaplane-rated pilot. On May 20, 2009, he became the first astronaut to stand on top of the world, the summit of Mount Everest. He is Founder and CEO of Fluidity Technologies, focused on the development of revolutionary input devices powered by machine learning to intuitively move through physical and virtual space. He also serves as Chief Medical Officer of Community Wellness, delivering state-of-the-art remote patient monitoring and wellness coaching to aging adults. Visit: www.parazynski.com and www.fluidity.tech

**Annie Evans (page 19)**

Annie Evans is an author, speaker, coach, and trainer focusing on helping people to become their best selves. She is also a California Realtor. Central to Annie's knowledge is the time she spent living at sea, logging 44,000 miles as celestial navigator on a 57' Catamaran throughout the Pacific. She has been a horse trainer, a celestial navigator, and has worked in fashion and architecture, project manager and business advisor, product developer, home/interior designer and international supply chain director (she took one start-up from $7million to $25million). She formed the William Parke Evans Foundation, a 501(c)3 in her late brother's name who succumbed to complications from mental illness. Visit www.SetYourSails.com

**Ruben Gonzalez (page 25)**

The first person to compete in four Winter Olympics each in a different decade, Ruben Gonzalez takes people's excuses away and inspires them to produce more than ever before. Ruben was the oldest luge competitor, who at the age of 47, competed in the Vancouver Olympics. At the age of 21, he decided to compete in the Olympics. He took up the sport of Luge and just four years later was racing for the gold against the best athletes in the world. He leveraged his strategy to create what are now time-tested techniques to excel in business today—to become unstoppable. He is a bestselling author and business and keynote speaker. Since 2002, Ruben has spoken for 100-plus Fortune 500 companies. Visit his website: TheLugeMan.com

**Bill Way (page 29)**

Live Free LLC was founded by Bill Way, CEO and owner, in October, 2009. The *Healthy Smart Mart*™ brand was created in 2018, although the company has been assisting clients in setting up profitable vending machine operations since 1988 under its former name, Freedom Technology. The company was originally founded by Bill in

March 1972, under the name Way & Associates, Inc. Bill Way is the best-selling author of *Vending Success Secrets – How anyone can grow rich in America's Best Cash Business!* in print since 1988 and now in its third edition. His next book is titled *Micro Markets – New Opportunities with Vending Gone Wild!* For more information, visit https://healthysmartmart.com

**Adam Edelstein (page 35)**

Since 1995, Adam Edelstein has worked on radio stations in upstate New York, Michigan, and Pennsylvania. In 2000, he landed his current job in Worcester, MA. Adam delivers morning news and hosts a morning show on a country music station, while simultaneously co-hosting the rock station down the hall. An avid hockey fan, Adam is the public address announcer at Worcester Railers (ECHL) hockey games. He performs stand-up comedy and owns Comedy for Cash Fundraising. Adam is a Senior Science Writer and content manager at the Diabetes Center of Excellence at UMass Medical School.

**Eric Power (page 40)**

Eric Louis Power served honorably in the United States Navy from 2002 to 2012, reaching the rank of Petty Officer First Class. He served in Operation Iraqi Freedom, Operation Enduring Freedom, and Operation Southern Watch. Eric has a total of seven deployments, with 3.5 years in Active Combat zones. A merchant at heart, Eric created

Veterans Disability Help, LLC while pursuing his first business degree. He is a co-author of the best-selling book, *Power of Proximity* and the author of *Don't Shoot Your Future Self* and *Be Kind to Your Future Self*. Eric was recently awarded a star of fame on Las Vegas Boulevard for his work within the veteran community and as an author. The city of Las Vegas dedicated Veterans Day, which is November 11th, as "Eric Power Day." Visit his website: https://veterandisabilityhelp.com/lions-den

**Kristoffer Doura (page 50)**

Kristoffer Doura learned the value of dedication at an early age growing up in Miami, FL, as the second of three children in an establishing immigrant home. Kristoffer's dedication, hard work, and determination to avoid a life of poverty and mediocrity inspired him to earn a Master's degree in Business Administration, leading to an accomplished financial services career. Kristoffer's career has been a model of service recognized throughout the South Florida community.

**Kari Petruch (page 54)**

Kari Petruch is a Master Relationship Coach, Strategic Interventionist, and Owner of Highest Intent Life Coaching. She is a mother of three and a grandmother of eight and is married to the man of her dreams. Having lived in many places in the world, she is uniquely qualified to help all people. Kari spent her young adulthood as a stay-at-home-mom, where she devoted herself to educating military families about the Individuals With Disabilities Act (IDEA) and volunteering as a parent advocate for children with special needs. Her truest mission is to help people embrace the incredible joy and excitement that comes with a great relationship so they will live their best lives together. In Kari's spare time, she volunteers her time to help military families have happier lives. She is the author of *Get Out of the Box and Into Play: The Secret to a Lasting Relationship*.

## James Blakemore (page 71)

James M. (Jim) Blakemore has an extensive, 40-year entrepreneurial career in several businesses and industries, including oil and gas, ranching, environmental remediation, marketing, radio broadcasting, banking, mining and natural resources, photography, building materials, direct marketing, and intellectual property, as well as real estate and other endeavors. He inspires and mentors people to success and helps them achieve outcomes well beyond what they believed possible. He currently serves as VP and Corporate Director at Primavera Resources of Dallas, TX, and is the Founder, President, and CEO of Bedford Falls Development of Midland, TX; and the Co-Founder, CEO, and Manager of EverGreen Manufacturing, LLC and J Cubed Workforce Housing, LLC. Jim is a Risk Management Specialist and is engaged in multiple ID Theft Awareness Programs. He serves on multiple charities, including the Blakemore Planetarium, The

Museum of the Southwest, The High Sky Children's Ranch, and Christmas in Action.

**David Stanley (page 77)**

David E. Stanley was born in Newport News, Virginia in 1955. Three years later, his parents divorced, setting the stage for an extraordinary event. In 1960, Dee Stanley married Vernon Presley, Elvis Presley's widowed father. David was just four years old, 20 years younger than his new stepbrother, when he moved into the Graceland Mansion in Memphis, TN. At the age of 16, David began working and touring with Elvis as a personal aide and bodyguard. From 1972 to 1977, he did hundreds of shows with his world-famous stepbrother. Today, David is a speaker, author, filmmaker, and the founder of Impello Entertainment, Inc. His published works the New York Times' bestseller, *Elvis: We Love You Tender*, *The Elvis Encyclopedia*, *Raised on Rock*, *Conversations with The King*, *Restoring My Father's Honor*, and his most recent release, *My Brother Elvis: The Final Years*. David also wrote, produced and directed the film *Protecting the King* in 2007 and is currently producing the TV drama-series *One of The Boys*.

**Phyllis Ayman (page 81)**

Phyllis Ayman is the "Ambassador for Aging Life Management" and founder of Mindful Longevity Solutions. Ayman created IMpathy®, an innovative program that addresses workforce burnout, fatigue, and overwhelm. Phyllis is a #1

Amazon bestselling author, speaker, panel moderator, and trainer. An eldercare advocate, speech/language pathologist, and dementia care specialist, she is a sought-after strategic advisor. Phyllis is the host of *SeniorsSTRAIGHTTalk*, a podcast on the Voice America Empowerment Channel and syndicated on the Voice America Influencers Channel. Visit her website: www.phyllisaymanassociates.com

**Mitch Axelrod (page 93)**

Mitchell Axelrod is founder of Axelrod & Associates, a business consulting firm and publisher of business and life skills books, training, workshops, and professional learning materials. Mitch has presented more than 3,500 seminars, workshops, keynotes, webinars, teleconferences, executive briefings and clinics to more than a million people on entrepreneurship, business, sales, marketing, values and life skills. He is the author of *The NEW Game of Business*™, *The NEW Game of IP*™ (Intellectual Property) and the #1 bestseller, *The NEW Game of Selling*™. Mitch is an intellectual property specialist and has taught classes at NYU, USC, and Notre Dame. He presented his newest work, "Values: The *Soul-Role-Goal* of Leadership™" at Harvard University's T.H. Chan School of Public Health. Mitch was presented with the Golden Mike Award® for speaking excellence and industry contribution.

## Alec Stern (page 98)

Sir Alec Stern has more than 25 years of experience as a founder, mentor, investor and hyper-growth agent for companies across various industries. He is an innovator with extensive expertise in growing and scaling companies, startup and operational growth, go-to-market strategy, strategic partnerships and more. As a primary member of Constant Contact's founding team, he was with the company for 18 years from start-up, to IPO, to a $1.1 Billion-Dollar acquisition. Alec was Knighted by the Royal Order of Constantine the Great and Saint Helen, of the Royal and Sovereign House of Cappadocia and San Bartolomeo. He is known as America's Startup Success Expert. Visit his website: http://www.alecspeaks.com

## Carlos Bueno (page 105(

Carlos Bueno is the Managing Director at The Newbury Boston, Boston's newest luxury hotel and one of the most legendary properties in the city. His career started at The Waldorf Astoria and led him to Four Seasons Hotels and Resorts, The Ritz-Carlton San Juan, The Plaza in New York, and the Fairmont Hotel Vancouver. In 2016, Mr. Bueno took the role of General Manager at the Taj Boston and has led the hotel through its lobby-to-roof renovation and transformation to become The Newbury Boston. Named Massachusetts Lodging Association's General Manager of the Year, he is active in the community and serves on the board of the Back Bay Association. Mr. Bueno resides in Brookline with his wife, two daughters, and labradoodle, Apollo.

**Peter Katz (page 110)**

Peter Katz is a JUNO Award and Canadian Screen Award-nominated singer-songwriter who has spent the past 15 years touring internationally. He has been described by many of his fans and speaking clients as "a thunderbolt for the soul." To date, his music has been streamed over 6 million times, and his music videos have over 21 million views on YouTube. Peter is also one of Canada's most in-demand speakers, acclaimed for giving highly customized "Keynote Concerts" to countless companies and organizations across various industries. For more information, contact info@peterkatzspeaks.com

**Greg Zlevor (page 118)**

Greg Zlevor is the President and Founder of Westwood International. He has over 25 years of experience in executive leadership development and education and has served as a coach, consultant, and facilitator for companies across Europe, Asia, North America, South America, and Australia. Under Greg's leadership, Westwood International has made it its mission to give back, supporting not-for-profit organizations that help homeless children and at-risk youth across the United States, Mexico, Thailand, India, and South America.

**Chris Naugle (page 122)**

From pro-snowboarder to money mogul, Chris Naugle has dedicated his life to being America's #1 Money Mentor. He has built and owned 20 companies, with his businesses being featured in Forbes, ABC, House Hunters, and his own HGTV pilot in 2018. He is currently founder of The Money School™, which teaches you to be your own bank and helps you solve your money problem by putting you in control of your money. His success also includes managing tens of millions of dollars in assets in the financial services and advisory industry and in real estate transactions. Chris is also a nationally recognized speaker, author, and podcast host. For more information, email Contact@ChrisNaugle.com

Made in the USA
Columbia, SC
14 April 2023

840fd144-57f5-4bab-b0de-b743f3a528b0R01